CAMP NAHGANO

Margina Sisson

13HORROR.COM BOOKS
An imprint of
DIZZY EMU PUBLISHING
1714 N McCadden Place, Hollywood, Los Angeles 90028
dizzyemupublishing.com

Camp Nahgano
Margina Sisson

First published in the United States
in 2022 by 13Horror.com Books

1 3 5 7 9 10 8 6 4 2

CAMP NAHGANO

Margina Sisson

CAMP NAHGANO

By

Margina Sisson

WGA# 2144235
red.writer@rocketmail.com

FADE IN:

EXT. TEHACHAPI MOUNTAINS - LATE AFTERNOON

A BACKPACKER and his WOLFDOG skillfully trudge along a steep incline of chaparral and manzanita. The backpacker, Native American, 30s and handsome, has a long braid down his back. Around his neck on a leather cord, a large wolf fang.

EXT. TEHACHAPI MOUNTAINS - DUSK

The backpacker and wolfdog sit before a crackling fire with their dome tent behind them. The flickering fire reflects onto the shiny knife he's sharpening. SCRAAPPEE.

A loud CRACK and a manzanita limb drops. The backpacker leaps to safety but his knife slices his hand in the process. Blood gushes.

BACKPACKER
(shocked)
What the hell?

He jumps over the limb and snatches up a small pouch. Pulls out a neckerchief and wraps his hand while looking upward.

BACKPACKER (CONT'D)
Manzanita doesn't snap like that.

Wolfdog whimpers.

BACKPACKER (CONT'D)
I'm okay. Just a scratch.

The wolfdog sniffs the air.

INT. TENT - NIGHT

Inside it's dark, quiet. The backpacker, cozy in his bag, sleeps. A woven dreamcatcher with feathers hangs above his head. His dog, curled up next to him has one eye open. The smoldering campfire visible through the fabric of the tent.

A POP and the dog sits up, sniffs, listens. Lowering his head he backs away from the zippered door, GROWLING. The backpacker wakes, quickly sits. Notices blood on his bag from his cut hand, then quickly turns his attention to his dog.

BACKPACKER
(whispering)
What's up Tala? Hear'n some 'em?

The dog GROWLS. The backpacker reaches for his flashlight and knife. He waits a moment, listening. It's quiet, nothing. He reaches for the tent door zipper, slowly unzips. ZIIPPPPP.

EXT. TENT - CONTINUOUS

He flicks on the flashlight creating an instant silhouette against the tent walls. Light floods from the unzipped open door onto the ground and brush outside.

Instantly SCREAMS cry out as he and his dog fight for their lives against something unseen. The dog YIPES rushes from the tent, the backpacker SCREAMS in pain.

A sudden BURST of blood and flesh explode inside the tent. The horrifying scene illuminated by the fallen flashlight reveals oozing matter against the tent walls. Off in the distance, a distraught HOWL from the wolfdog, then silence.

A low CRACKLING noise begins from inside the tent. It becomes louder and louder as the blood and flesh are eaten away by something, leaving behind the jagged words; CAMP NAHGANO.

DISSOLVE TO:

EXT. MOUNTAIN ROAD - AFTERNOON

Haunted-sounding theme music PLAYS as a large van, roof racks and luggage on top, makes its way up a curvy two-lane road. On the side, a spirit-themed sign for "SPIRIT HUNTERS".

The MUSIC continues for this now obvious intro into a Spirit Hunter show, introducing each of the seven INVESTIGATORS. The promo is snappy and professional as these ghost hunters use the best ghost hunting devices and equipment money can buy.

The short intro video suddenly JUMPS. The music STOPS and the image FREEZES. PULL BACK to see it's on a computer screen.

INT. VAN - AFTERNOON - CONTINUOUS

PULL BACK to see the computer screen is in the back of a van. At the computer, CHUCK, 20s, headphone around his neck, looks up.

CHUCK

Yo Rob! I'm trying to edit here.

UP FRONT

ROB, early 30s the driver and SAMANTHA, riding shotgun, a curvy brunette, late 20s looks back. We recognize them both as Investigators from the video intro we just saw.

ROB
Sorry.

She looks over at Rob.

SAMANTHA
I told you we shoulda stayed on the main road.

ROB
And we'd still be sitting behind that overturned big rig. Like I said, this shortcut's gonna cut our drive time in half. Isn't that what you wanted?

SAMANTHA
And once again you think you know what's best for everyone (beat) and if it's such a great shortcut, how come nobody else is taking it?

She turns away, resumes watching the scenery swoosh by. He glances over into his side mirror. POV of the side-mirror to see no other vehicles behind them.

ROB (O.C.)
Our gain their loss.

IN BACK

It's a ghost hunter command center with state-of-the-art monitors and equipment. We recognize everyone from the show.

In the far back, Chuck rolls a joint while dead-pan TOM, late 20s, fiddles with an impressive camera. Near the middle, KEVIN, 20s, perfect hair and dimples, digs through a cooler.

KEVIN
Any one else hungry?

KAT, 20s, stunning with dark-skin and brown eyes, looks up from the yellow-lined pad she's writing in.

KAT
How the hell do you stay so thin?

KEVIN
Good metabolism. Among other amazing attributes.

JULIE, 20s, an O C beach blonde looks up from her laptop.

JULIE
And what might those be?

CHUCK
Ohh no. Here we go.

TOM
Don't even get him started.

KAT
I second that.

Chuck lights the joint, takes a hit.

KEVIN
I'm just say'n, you need to learn from the master.

JULIE
And you're the master?

Chuck passes the joint to Tom. Kevin continues digging.

TOM
(laughing)
More like master of none.

KEVIN
Dude, give it a rest.

Tom shrugs, takes a hit, offers to Kevin who declines. Chuck takes it back, then blows smoke out his chipped front tooth.

JULIE
Ewe, that's gross.

KEVIN
(toward Julie)
Anyway Julie, you'd think with all this trick equipment we'd find some real ghosts. So someone has to pretend. Therefore I'm the master.

KAT
You're not the whole show, Kevin.

KEVIN
Most of it. Of course now Julie's on board so we'll see.

CHUCK
(laughing)
If you ever saw a real ghost?

KEVIN
I'd run like hell, that's what.

They all LAUGH. Kevin finds his sandwich, unwraps, enjoys. Chuck offers the joint to Julie.

JULIE
Get that shit outta my face.

She waves the smoke away. Chuck continues to hold it out.

CHUCK
Come on. It'd be good for you.

JULIE
(toward Rob)
Rob, your little brother's being a dick again.

ROB
Chuck. Chill the fuck out will ya?

CHUCK
What do you think I'm trying to do.

SAMANTHA
Hey, you gonna bogart that joint?

KAT
When did you start smoking?

The joint gets passed to Sam. She takes a hit, COUGHS. Turns to see Rob's shocked look, then passes it back. Tom watches.

JULIE
(toward Kevin)
So wait a minute, this equipment thing. I thought it was all fake props but you're saying we could find real ghosts because the equipment is real?

KEVIN
If you believe in that sort of shit which a lot of people do but I've never seen one. Thank God.

TOM
Nor have I, since I debunk just about everything.

JULIE
You're no fun.

KEVIN
Basically it's down to perception. With our state-of-the-art equipment and my masterful acting-

CHUCK
-My editing and special effects.

KEVIN
Suddenly we're more credible and credibility gets customers.

ROB (O.S.)
And customers equal, Cha-Ching.

JULIE
Well if it makes my sizzle-reel even more legit, then hell yeah!

ROB (O.S.)
Hey Kev, pass me my sandwich.

Kevin digs and finds the ziplock with ROB's sandwich. It's squishy. He passes it forward to Sam who passes it to Rob.

SAMANTHA
Ewe.

KEVIN
What's with your sandwiches bro?

ROB
I happen to like rare lunchmeat.

KEVIN
You mean bloody.

ROB
It's not bloody.

SAMANTHA
It's disgusting, that's what it is.

Rob ignores her as he unwraps, takes a fews bites then puts it down on a pile of white paper towels on the dash when-

POP! The van shutters and leans left. A collective GASP from everyone in back.

ROB
Hold on, we gotta flat.

SAMANTHA
Great. What else.

EXT. TEHACHAPI MOUNTAIN ROAD - AT THAT MOMENT

The van limps to a stop. Rob jumps out, heads toward the back. The sliding-door on the other side is HEARD opening.

Rob stands behind the van assessing the damage when the others arrive. Kat shows up, takes in the surroundings.

CHUCK
Damn bro, this is bad.

ROB
Yeah well, let's get the spare and change it out. We gotta keep mov'n.

CHUCK
I didn't pack the spare.

ROB
WHAT?!

Tom puts his arm over Chuck's shoulder.

TOM
Son. That was not a good move.

SAMANTHA
Great, we're never getting to Tehachapi by nightfall now.

ROB
Frick'n perfect.

CHUCK
I got this.

ROB
Yeah right.

Chuck opens the back van doors revealing a box full of stuff.

ROB (CONT'D)
(toward Samantha)
See if you can find a campground?

SAMANTHA
What, we gonna walk?

Tom chuckles.

ROB
Samantha. Just find one.

She sarcastically salutes. Rob frowns, walks away, steaming.

KEVIN
(looks around)
Anyone have triple A?

EXT. BACK OF VAN

Chuck rummages through a box. Sam digs in the cooler, finds a Coke, drinks. Kat jots down notes in her notepad.

CHUCK
It's not like the end of the world.

JULIE
What about those scary movies where they break down and everyone dies.

She looks around.

JULIE (CONT'D)
I mean, look at this place.

TOM
Good idea, I should start filming.

She slugs Tom's arm, he LAUGHS.

Sam leans against a tree searching for campgrounds on her cellphone while Chuck pulls out a yellow aerosol can.

CHUCK
See, you guys are all whipped up over nothing. I brought this. It's fix-a-flat. Eight bucks on Amazon.

KEVIN
I love Amazon.

Rob returns more cooled down. He shakes his head, SIGHS.

ROB
Well, at least that might get it off the rim.

CHUCK
That's what I was trying to tell you. But I also have this.

He grabs a yellow handled case about the size of a radio.

CHUCK (CONT'D)
It's a tire inflater compressor.

TOM
Now we're talk'n.

ROB
I suppose you charged my card?

JULIE
Who cares. Let's fix and go.

EXT. SIDE OF ROAD - LATER

The compressor slowly fills the tire as-

Rob wanders, deep thinking. Kevin sunbathes on a rock using foil. Sam scrolls in her cellphone as Tom shoots b-roll footage. Tom rotates his camera to Sam. She looks up, smiles. He wanders over.

Kat sits off nearby writing in her pad. Julie just stands there taking everything in, slightly nervous.

Sam and Tom now engaged in conversation, glance over at Rob.

Chuck, working the compressor gets a nose bleed. He touches his finger up under his nose. Blood.

CHUCK
Shit. Not again.

He pinches his nose, drops his head back. Kevin looks up.

KEVIN
What, is this like your third one?

CHUCK
Forth. But who's counting.

SAMANTHA
That's not good.

CHUCK
I used to get 'em all the time as a kid but haven't had one for years.

TOM
Maybe you're in menopause.

Sam GIGGLES.

CHUCK
Oh that's funny.

KEVIN
You might need a transfusion.

JULIE
What?

KAT
He's kidding.

TOM
Thought you were supposed to put your head between your knees.

JULIE
He's not crashing in an airplane Tom, he's got a nose bleed.

CHUCK
I'll be fine. It's nothing.

Julie hands Chuck a wad of tissues. He's thankful. She then wanders over to Kat.

JULIE
Hey Kat. You work'n on the Script?

Kat NODS.

KAT
It's for the old Southern Pacific Railroad Depot, built back in 1904 but on tracks from 1876, so we wanna lot of old train references.

JULIE
Like what?

KAT
Oh like, throttle, conductor, derail. Stuff like that. It's for the spirit box or should I say, Kevin, voice actor extraordinaire.

KEVIN (O.S.)
Now we're talk'n.

They LAUGH. Julie notices Kat's necklace.

JULIE
That is so trippy. Is it a tooth?

KAT
A wolf fang actually.

Kat holds up her leather corded necklace with a wolf fang.

JULIE
Whoa, where did you get that?

KAT
My Grandmother passed away last month and this necklace was in her safety-deposit box with a note that read, "A match from the past comes together to save our future."

JULIE
What's that supposed to mean?

KAT
I'm not sure but I love it and never take it off.

JULIE
Cool. So you're Native American.

KAT
Ka-waii-su, on my Mom's side.

JULIE
Kaw-wai what?

KAT
(laughing)
Kawaiisu. Actually from right around these mountains.

JULIE
And what about your Dad?

KAT
Never knew my dad.

JULIE
I'm sorry.

KAT
It's okay. My Mom passed when I was eight so my grandma raised me. She would never talk about my dad.
(MORE)

KAT (CONT'D)
Even when I asked. Now she's gone so I guess I'll never know.

JULIE
You should totally do a D N A.

KAT
I've always wanted to.

An eagle circles and soars above them. Julie notices.

JULIE
Is that an eagle?

KAT
(looking up)
Sure is. Soaring Eagle. That's what they used to call my mom.

JULIE
Maybe she's looking out for you.

Kat smiles.

SAMANTHA (O.S.)
Hey guys, I found a place to camp super close. Oak Pine campground.

KAT
Sounds good to me.

CHUCK
I'm down with that.

Chuck tosses his bloody tissues down onto the ground.

ROB
Hey slob. Pick those up.

CHUCK
Like anyone's gonna care.

KAT
Mother Nature does.

Chuck hastily picks up the bloody tissues.

CHUCK
Whatever.

ROB
So the campground. How far is it?

SAMANTHA
A couple miles up.

JULIE
Hot shower here I come.

SAMANTHA
(toward Tom)
And, it'll still be early enough to get some beauty shots.

She strikes a few sexy poses toward Tom who now focuses his camera on her, smiling. Rob notices, clears his throat.

ROB
Chuck, we almost done here?

INT. VAN - LATER

As soon as the van pulls back onto the road it instantly sputters and stalls. Rob, just about to take a bite, puts his sandwich back down on the pile of now reddish paper towels.

ROB
What the hell.

SAMANTHA
Half the time, huh?

ROB
I don't wanna hear it, Sam.

Rob puts it in neutral, coasts down the slight hill to a turn-off. Throws it into park, tries the key and VROOM. It starts.

ROB (CONT'D)
I'm gonna keep going.

Everyone agrees. He begins to pull away when he stops again.

ROB (CONT'D)
Hey, what about this?

Out the window they see an old weathered sign for CAMP NAHGANO (NAH-GAN-NO) advertising Lodging and Hot Showers a mile up the road. Samantha looks back at her cellphone.

SAMANTHA
Camp Nahgano? It's not even on here.

JULIE
Who cares, they have hot showers!

TOM
From the looks of that sign you'll
be lucky to get water.

JULIE
Whatever.

ROB
Okay, so we're gonna try it?

EXT. TEHACHAPI MOUNTAIN ROAD

As soon as the van pulls away heading toward Camp Nahgano, the weathered sign instantly disintegrates and floats away.

INT. VAN

Rob concentrates on driving. Sam sees another sign, points.

SAMANTHA
Looks like we're turning left.

Rob turns left onto a less traveled road. It suddenly becomes unnaturally dark. The road, half-paved continues until-

JULIE
Look, there it is!

Rob pulls up to the entrance. Everyone looks out the window to see the worn and cockeyed entrance to CAMP NAHGANO.

SAMANTHA
This is it?

ROB
We do have a small problem tho.

He points.

ROB (CONT'D)
There is the matter of the chain.

Out the window they see a large rusted chain pulled tight across the entrance with an antique lock holding it shut.

SAMANTHA
Well, that's that.

KEVIN
What do you mean that's that.

SAMANTHA
It's private property, Kevin. We can't just break in. Let's go back and find the real campground.

ROB
(agreeable)
While the engine's still running.

JULIE
You're the one that drove us down here. Now you're gonna let a little chain stop us? Where's your sense of adventure? And aren't we supposed to be ghost hunters? Plus the engine hasn't cut out once since we got here.

KAT
She's right. We should go in.

ROB
You're agreeing with the newbie?
(toward Julie)
No offense.

Julie shrugs. Chuck lights another joint. Passes to Tom.

TOM
Whoa, I really don't need breaking and entering on my record.

KAT
Look, I don't know why but I feel compelled to check it out. Besides, look at that chain and lock. The weeds. No one's been here for eons. And just think, maybe with all this trick equipment we'll finally catch-

KEVIN
-Don't say it.

CHUCK
Yes! Wanna see Kevin run like hell.

KEVIN
(under his breath)
Ass hat.

SAMANTHA
Look, I'm sorry but we don't even know what's in there. So breaking in private property for nothing.

JULIE
Might not be nothing. We could make this another episode.

TOM
I'm down with that.

ROB
Okay well, we gotta make a decision. Now or never.

Everyone waits for Samantha.

SAMANTHA
Fine.

JULIE
Excellent! So how we gonna get in?

CHUCK
Hell, I got the tool for that.

Chuck flips open the latches on a large tool box.

INT. LARGE ROOM - SOMEWHERE - DAY

A bright control-room with wall-mounted monitors and a panel of flickering lights, gears and levers. A SCOREBOARD of sorts hangs prominently on the wall. It reads; 993. At the other end of the room, an extra long bed and table for one.

A stark white, bald-headed TALL MAN, dressed in a black suit peers out the curtained window.

A TAP at the door, it opens revealing HALBERT, a sheepish attentive man under the tall man's employ. The tall man continues his gaze out the window.

HALBERT
Sir? You wanted to see me?

The tall man whips around revealing his pale features, small blue-tinted goggles and a mouth so unnaturally wide it hurts.

TALL MAN
(cheerful)
Halbert. Today is a great day, yes?

HALBERT
(confused)
It is?

TALL MAN
Of course it is. How long have we been at it now. Huh?

HALBERT
(thinking)
Well uh.

TALL MAN
Don't answer. Makes me feel old.

The tall man runs his hand along the scoreboard, caressing.

TALL MAN (CONT'D)
But Halbert, a great day indeed.

HALBERT
If you say so.

Tall man whips back around as his face hideously contorts. His lips draw back exposing rows of jagged teeth. He SNARLS.

TALL MAN
Make sure the grounds are perfect.

HALBERT
But sir, they already look-

TALL MAN
(anger)
-I said perfect!

His lips instantly recede back to normal.

TALL MAN (CONT'D)
(nice again)
We're having guests. Oh, and start rationing the food for everyone.

HALBERT
But we're already rationing.

Tall man leans in.

TALL MAN
Then ration more.

HALBERT
Yes sir, right away sir.

Halbert quickly backs out of the room. The door closes.

The tall man turns back toward the monitor where the van is seen idling at the front chain entrance.

EXT. CAMP NAHGANO ENTRANCE

The van idles as Chuck approaches the rusted chain and lock. A quick snip and the lock and chain fall to the ground.

As he kicks aside the lock, he notices a white chalky line across the entrance that continues along the property line. He drags his boot through the chalky substance, spreading it.

CHUCK
Humph.

EXT. CAMP NAHGANO ENTRANCE - A MOMENT LATER

The van drives over the chain and white substance. As soon as the back tires pass the broken chain entrance, the chain and lock reappear across the entrance as if never being cut.

The van picks up speed along the partially-paved road.

INT. VAN - CONTINUOUS

Rob drives. THUMP! The van rocks hard to the right. Kat whips around looking back through her window, catches a glimpse of a bloody deer falling to the ground.

KAT
Oh my God, you just hit a deer!

He slams on the brakes. Throws it into park. His partially eaten sandwich still on a pile of pink paper towels.

ROB
I didn't even see it! Damn it!

He unbuckles his seat belt.

SAMANTHA
Where are you going?

ROB
Gotta see the damage. You know I'm leasing this van. Damn it. Last thing I need is an insurance hike.

He exits. Kat unbuckles, slides open the door.

KEVIN
Now where are you going?

KAT
To find that deer, it's hurt.

JULIE
And then what.

KAT
It's a live animal, Julie.

JULIE
I don't wanna see half-dead Bambi.

KAT
Where's your sense of adventure?

Kat hops out. Julie rolls her eyes. Tom unbuckles.

TOM
I should film this.

Kevin, Sam, Julie and Chuck all unbuckle.

EXT. VAN - SIDE OF ROAD

The van idles as Rob and Kevin evaluate the dent and broken headlight. CLOSE to see where the headlight lens broke off.

Everyone else is out. Chuck takes a piss behind a tree, Julie and Sam chat it up as Tom heads toward Kat with his camera.

In the foreground, Rob's sandwich is instantly overtaken by billions of ants, consuming it in seconds. Nobody notices.

EXT. CRASH SITE - SIDE OF ROAD

Kat stands just off the road, looking down. Tom films his arrival. He pans the camera down and around.

TOM
So it ran off?

KAT
I don't think so.

TOM
What do you mean. Where is it?

Kat points downward. Tom films. POV from the camera moving down to see a perfectly intact skeleton of a deer.

TOM (O.C.) (CONT'D)
Why exactly am I looking at this?

KAT (O.C.)
It's the deer. The one we hit. I saw it fall right here.

TOM (O.C.)
Usually when they run across the road it's more than bones. Just say'n. Thanks for the footage tho.

He turns to leave. Kat notices something, crouches down.

KAT
Hey wait a minute. What's this?

He turns back. CLOSE as she tugs at a large shard of plastic lodged in the animals eye socket. Another tug, she pulls it free, holds it up just as Rob and Kevin arrive.

ROB
Hey, you found my broken lens.

Kat and Tom share a confused look. Up above, the eagle soars.

INT. VAN - A MOMENT LATER

Back in the van, Rob throws it into gear, drives on.

ROB
There goes my insurance.

CHUCK
Just don't turn it in.

KAT
I still don't get how that broken lens ended up in those bones.

TOM
Obviously the deer hit us, broken lens landed on the bones, wah lah.

KAT
You saw it yourself Tom, it was *in* the bone not on it. Explain that?

Rob reaches for his sandwich, it's gone.

ROB
Hey, where's my sandwich? It was just here. All right, who took it. Samantha?

SAMANTHA
I didn't take it.

ROB
Tom?

TOM
(sarcastic)
Seriously?

ROB
It was right here.

SAMANTHA
Well who ever took it...

She picks up a clean white paper towel.

SAMANTHA (CONT'D)
...Left a clean one.

KAT
That's weird.

ROB
Chuck, if you're pranking me, now is NOT the time.

CHUCK
Trust me, I swear. I am not pranking you. I did not take it.

KAT
Another mystery and we're not even there yet.

She quickly scribbles in her note pad. Rob leans forward.

ROB
Hey. You guys seeing this?

EXT. CAMP NAHGANO ROAD

The van drives across an old wooden bridge with the rushing river below. Then passes a series of faded signs welcoming guests to Camp Nahgano.

Larger-than-life rusted Indian arrows protrude from the ground as if propelled by giants leading the way. An abandoned play area with the skeletal remains of huts.

JULIE (V.O.)
This is majorly creepy.

TOM (V.O.)
Majorly creepy's good for business.

INT. VAN

Rob drives slow. Everyone watches out the windows.

KAT
For some reason, it feels so familiar. Like I've been here.

SAMANTHA
Maybe as a kid. Summer camp?

KAT
I don't know, maybe not.

JULIE
I wonder what Nahgano even means. Is it like a tribe or something?

KAT
No tribe I ever heard of. I think the word Nah-gah means, to meet.

The van rolls up to a dilapidated two-story log cabin lodge. Everyone peers out the window at the graffiti covered porch with a boarded up entrance that now appears pried open.

Instant CHEERS of excitement fill the van.

KEVIN
Bonus gig!

CHUCK
Cha Ching!

KAT
Better than I expected.

JULIE
Still think it's nothing, Sam.

Sam SHRUGS.

ROB
This place *is* promising.

TOM
Holy shit Sam. We can set up the I.R. Cameras, rim pods, voice recorders, spirit box, everything!

SAMANTHA
Hold up cowboy, we're only here one night.

ROB
Yeah, hold up cowboy.

TOM
(serious at Samantha)
I'd be happy with one night.

Her eyes WIDEN. Chuck peers out the window.

CHUCK
Maybe we'll get lucky.

SAMANTHA
(toward Tom)
Maybe we will.

Rob throws the van into park with a JOLT.

EXT. CAMP NAHGANO LODGE ENTRANCE - LATER

The van sits in between the lodge and the rushing river. Everyone is out stretching their legs and looking around.

ROB
Okay, I want the tents over there, Tom you go get firewood, then help Chuck pull cables. Kat, Sam and Julie, help Kevin set up camp. Chop chop, we only got an hour and a half of daylight left.

CHUCK
Why are we camping out here again when we could be in there?

Chuck smacks the side of his neck to kill a bug.

ROB
(upset)
Because we don't even know what's in there yet! End of discussion!

KEVIN
(toward Chuck)
Safety first Boy Scout.

Rob heads toward the lodge, Sam watches. Kat and Kevin look for tent spots. Tom collects wood. Julie leans into Chuck.

JULIE
(under her breath)
What's up with your brother?

CHUCK
I think he's pissed about the van.
Or that stupid sandwich. Or both.

Chuck grabs a roll of cable. Julie grabs a sleeping bag.

JULIE
I think he's pissed about Tom.

CHUCK
What about Tom?

Julie lowers her voice.

JULIE
He was just hitting on Sam, how did you not see that? And she was dig'n it. So she and Rob broke up? Cause when they interviewed me they were-

CHUCK
-It's been back and forth. I actually thought they just got back together until I heard Sam say'n after Tehachapi she's gone.

JULIE
Ooh drama.

CHUCK
Yeah, but keep it on the down-low.

She makes a 'zip up your lips' motion.

KAT (O.S.)
Hey Julie, grab the tent stakes.

Julie reaches for the tent stake bag.

EXT. CAMP NAHGANO LODGE - CAMPGROUND - LATE AFTERNOON

The rushing river flows just below the cliff where they set up two large tents and folding chairs. The van sits close by. Chuck attaches a mic onto Julie. Sam giggles and flirts with Tom. Kat holds a clipboard. Rob arrives with flashlights.

ROB
Okay everyone listen up.

Everyone stops what they're doing except for Sam who GIGGLES.

ROB (CONT'D)
(toward Sam)
You wanna be a part of this?

She stops giggling and pays attention.

ROB (CONT'D)
Okay, I did a quick walk-around and this place hasn't had anyone in it for I'm gonna say, decades. That's the good news. Bad news is we haven't been inside or upstairs so we run it like we did the old farmhouse. Slow and cautious. Watch for loose floorboards, stay alert.
(toward Sam)
And as always, we need to look professional and legit.
(toward everyone)
Got it? Alright, let's use everything we got and maybe catch some real-

KEVIN
-Don't say it!

They LAUGH.

ROB
(toward Kat)
What are we calling this episode?

KAT
Camp Naugahyde. So we don't get sued.

ROB
Good thinking. Okay, carry on.

Kat hands both Kevin and Julie a piece of paper.

KAT
Here's your scripts. Obviously we have to improvise, especially since this lodge was built on top of,
(looking upward)
An old Indian burial ground. And trust me, they're not happy.

JULIE
(convinced)
Oh my God, Really?

KAT
Not really. I just made that up.

The group LAUGHS. Everyone begins moving toward the lodge.

JULIE
Holy fucking shit, she's good.

CHUCK
Don't make me bleep you.

A curtain in an upstairs window MOVES. No one notices.

Rob hangs back.

ROB
Hey Sam, can I see you a second?

Samantha, seemingly annoyed, heads toward Rob. Julie and Chuck pay extra attention. Rob moves further from earshot.

Sam arrives to where Rob is waiting.

SAMANTHA
What.

ROB
You know how I feel about you. And it's obvious how you feel about me.

SAMANTHA
And?

ROB
Just wait until after Tehachapi before you throw it in my face.

He turns, walks toward the others. She's caught off guard.

KEVIN (O.C.)
We do'n this?

ROB
Let's go.

Tom FLICKS on his camera. Rob straps on his Go-Pro chest cam.

INT. VAN - DUSK

In the back, Chuck sits amid monitors and instruments. He throws on his headphones, lights a joint. He flips a switch. Instantly the monitor lights up, shows Tom's camera POV.

CHUCK
And away we go.

He pops open a window.

EXT. CAMP NAHGANO LODGE - FRONT PORCH - SUNDOWN

Tom has the camera trained on both Kevin and Julie. Camera POV CLOSE on the clap-board.

KAT (O.C.)
Spirit Hunters, episode six.

SNAP! Camera POV on Kevin and Julie. Into the camera.

KEVIN
Hey everyone, Kevin McAlester here along with new investigator-

JULIE
Julie Carter for another episode of-

KEVIN
Spirit Hunters.

JULIE (CONT'D)
Spirit Hunters.

KEVIN (CONT'D)
We're at probably the most haunted site we've ever been and I'd be lying to say I'm not excited.

Camera pans the porch. A chalky line runs over the threshold.

JULIE
Welcome to camp Naugahyde. This place is off the chart creepy and we're not even through the door.

KEVIN
And, it's a big place so we'll be investigating with the entire team.

Camera PANS showing Kat, Sam and Rob. Tom pops his face into frame, then PANS over toward Chuck in the van, who waves. Camera POV back to Kevin and Julie.

KEVIN (CONT'D)
So let's get started...

They each hold a ghost hunting device and flashlight.

INT. VAN - SAME

Chuck monitors the group on screen from Tom's camera as they prepare to enter. He grabs his walkie-talkie.

CHUCK
This is base camp. Over.

ROB (V.O.)
(through walkie-talkie)
Okay base, we're heading in.

CHUCK
Copy that. Hey Rob? I don't see your feed yet?

ROB (V.O.)
(through walkie-talkie)
I'll kick it on once we start.

CHUCK
Sounds good.

Chuck puffs on the joint, blows the smoke out the window.

EXT. CAMP NAHGANO CAMPSITE - VAN - SAME

The van, lit by lights inside, creates an eerie aura around it. It's dead quiet outside. Not even a cricket. Chuck's puff of smoke floats upward where the eagle soars above the van.

INT. CAMP NAHGANO LODGE - FIRST FLOOR

POV of Tom's camera from behind as everyone enters. It's dark. They flip on their flashlights, scan the room. Cobwebs stream from the ceiling down to the sheet-draped furniture. Everything appears undisturbed. Julie hacks through the webs.

JULIE
Talk about neglect.

Rob shines his flashlight across the grand room toward a large fireplace with a mounted buffalo head.

ROB
Check that out.

KEVIN
Yo, get a shot of me by that.

Kevin b-lines to the fireplace as Tom follows.

ROB
Guys, let's get this set up first.

Tom takes a quick shot of Kevin before heading back with the group. The mounted buffalo's eyes move to watch them go.

ROB (CONT'D)
Okay, we'll cover more ground if we split up so, Tom, Kat and Julie set up the I.R's, spirit box and grid down here. Me, Sam and Kevin will plant voice recorders and one I.R for the hallway upstairs. Good?

SAMANTHA
(to Rob)
I'm hang'n down here with Julie.

ROB
Whatever. Then Kat's with me.

Rob flicks on his chest-cam, grabs his walkie-talkie.

ROB (CONT'D)
(into walkie-talkie)
Hey Chuck. We're starting.

CHUCK (V.O.)
(through walkie-talkie)
Copy that. I see your feed. Over.

The team splits up. Rob's flashlight shines up the staircase.

INT. LODGE - 1ST FLOOR

POV from Tom's camera on Samantha and Julie as they stand in front of the fireplace. The buffalo seems to watch. Julie takes another glance at her script then NODS she's ready.

The open clapboard appears in frame held by Tom.

TOM (O.C.)
Camera and sound rolling. Camp Naugahyde, scene two.

He closes it, SNAP. Camera POV on Sam and Julie.

SAMANTHA
So we've done some research and found that this lodge was built in nineteen forty-five on top of an old ancient Indian burial ground.

JULIE
Supposedly the lodge owner claimed they had no knowledge of that, but when more and more unexplained deaths kept occurring here, they claimed the lodge was cursed, closed it and walked away forever.

SAMANTHA
And as you can see, this place looks more like a hunters lodge than something representing the indigenous people who once lived here. Kinda shameful really.

JULIE
KINDA. What a bunch of a-holes. Oops, can I say that?

TOM (O.S.)
A-holes? Yeah.

Julie appears startled.

JULIE
Whoa, did you just feel that?

She holds out her temperature meter. CLOSE on temp falling.

JULIE (CONT'D)
Oh my God the temperature literally just dropped like seven degrees.

SAMANTHA
Look at my hair.

The hair on her head and arms are standing straight up.

JULIE
Oh my God, your hair!

SAMANTHA
Look at the buffalo!

The buffalo's fur is now standing straight up. The buffalo's eyes appear wide open as if shocked.

TOM (O.S.)
That buffalo's eyes are crazy.

They all look up at the buffalo's eyes.

SAMANTHA
Do his eyes look different?

JULIE
Oh like I know him sooo well.

SAMANTHA
No seriously. Do they?

JULIE
And I seriously say, shut that thing off Tom, I hate this feeling.

Tom picks up a small box, flips a switch and the static that raised the hair on their head and arms instantly stops.

SAMANTHA
Thank you.

TOM
That was a good take.

JULIE
Come on, let's explore some more.

The three head toward the Kitchen.

INT. LODGE - 2ND FLOOR

POV from Rob's Go-Pro as Kevin and Kat cautiously walk the creaky hallway shining their flashlights through the webs.

KAT
We should put the I.R at the end of the hall pointing this direction.

ROB (O.C.)
Perfect. Kevin, let's do an E.V.P.

KEVIN
Oh, we're rolling? Cool. Okay.
(into Rob's Go-Pro)
We're on the second floor, about to place an I.R camera in the hallway. I.R or Infrared, identifies unusual heat signatures thought to be emitted by ghosts as energy.

He places the camera facing the hallway. A green light is on.

KAT
We'll also be putting voice recorders in a few of the rooms but first, let's do an E.V.P session.

KEVIN
E V P or Electro Voice Phenomena recorders pick up voices we otherwise can't hear with our ears.

Kat holds the device outward.

KAT
My name is Kat and this here is Rob and Kevin (pause) We're not here to harm you (pause) Would you like to speak with us today? (pause) What is your name? (pause)

She rewinds the RECORDING and plays it back, listening.

RECORDING
(from recorder)
We're not here to harm you (silence) Would you like to speak with us today? (silence) What is your name?

No responses. She flicks the recorder off. Nods to Rob.

ROB
Perfect, we'll add Kevin's voiceover in post. Let's do another E.V.P in the last room but first, a reaction shot starting from, what is your name?

Kat rewinds the recorder back a bit. Rob films her.

RECORDING
What is your name?

Kevin and Kat both look at each other, mouths open, shocked.

KEVIN
What was that?

KAT
That was awesome!

ROB
Cut. Perfect.

INT. VAN

CLOSE on the monitor where multiple camera views are in grid format. CLOSE on the grid showing Tom's camera POV as they approach the dining area.

INT. LODGE - FIRST FLOOR - SAME

Tom's camera POV of Samantha and Julie walking into an eerily dark dining area. The round sheet-covered tables seem normal compared to the chairs. All of which are curiously stacked floor to ceiling like crazy chair totem poles.

JULIE
That's interesting. How'd they get 'em up there?

The camera PANS upward to see the unusual sight.

TOM (O.S.)
Looks like something Chuck would do.

SAMANTHA
That's for sure.

Tom pulls out his walkie-talkie. Presses the button.

TOM
(into walkie-talkie)
Yo Chuck. You seeing this?

Tom PANS the camera again. The radio CRACKLES.

TOM (CONT'D)
(into walkie-talkie)
Hey man, not hearing you but I got this shot. Cool huh? Over and out.

SAMANTHA
Over and out?

TOM
That's what you're supposed to say.

JULIE
That's a big ten four good buddy.

The girls GIGGLE.

TOM
(toward Samantha)
Now, you're being naughty.

Sam blushes.

JULIE
What's this?

Julie B-lines to something big covered by a sheet. She WHIPS the sheet back producing a thick billowing cloud of dust that lands all over her. Her hair, face, clothes. Everything.

She COUGHS! COUGHS!

SAMANTHA
Holy shit. You're covered in it.

Julie bends forward, vigorously shakes dust from her hair. She whips her hair back and tries wiping her face.

JULIE
(spitting)
This is just grand.

She motions toward the piano, LAUGHING.

JULIE (CONT'D)
Get it? Grand piano?

SAMANTHA
Oh brother.

JULIE
Now I *do* need a shower.

TOM
Not until we finish. We still got the spirit box to do.

JULIE
I'm not look'n like this.

TOM
Okay, group shower.

JULIE
Yeah right. In your dreams.

Julie touches the piano key making a LOUD off-key TUNE.

SAMANTHA
Shhhhh.

JULIE
Why are you shushing? No ones here.

INT. VAN

Chuck gets interference on his screen and headphones. He pulls the headphones off, inspects the connection then puts them back on again, turning dials. He quickly yanks the headphones off again, shocked.

CHUCK
(confused)
What the hell?

Putting them back on to listen, his nose begins bleeding. He reaches up, touches. Yep, it's blood.

CHUCK (CONT'D)
Damn it! Frick'n great.

He pinches his nose while searching for tissues. CLOSE on the blood as it drops to the GROUND. DRIP!!!

EXT. CAMP NAHGANO - SOMEWHERE - SAME

Outside not far off, a large cone-shaped anthill sits abandoned, dormant, until a thick ribbon of ants burst from the spout like a lava flow of ants heading somewhere fast.

INT. LODGE - SECOND FLOOR - SAME

Exiting one of the rooms they are back in the hall making their way toward the last room. As they walk, faces protrude from the wallpaper and glide along unnoticed behind them.

Rob shines his flashlight on the last room, the only one with a closed door.

ROB
Figures.

They slowly approach. Kat senses something, whips around shining her flashlight. Faces are gone. She resumes forward.

Kevin hangs back, glances into a large mirror on the wall, fixes his hair. He doesn't notice the tall man staring down.

Rob puts his ear against the closed door, listening. It's all quiet. He looks down, scrapes his boot through the thick dust covering the floor.

ROB (CONT'D)
No ones been here forever.

He tries the door knob, it's locked.

INT. VAN - SAME

The instruments in front of Chuck have awakened with flashing lights and audible tones. The monitor showing Rob and Tom's cam views as well as the I.R camera setups, are now static. His nose still bleeding, bloody tissues are everywhere.

EXT. CAMP NAHGANO - SUNSET

The thick river of ants glide along rocks, past trees heading directly toward the van that's seen in the distance.

INT. LODGE - SECOND FLOOR

Rob stands at the closed door, pulls a Swiss Army knife from his pocket, searches. His Go-Pro battery BEEPS then dies.

ROB
Damn it, this is the second one dead. And that was my spare.

KAT
Don't worry. I'll go get another. But don't go in until I'm back.

ROB
Better hurry then.

His walkie-talkie CRACKLES. He picks it up. Kat waits.

ROB (CONT'D)
Base camp you try'n to reach me?

STATIC. Then, as if coming in waves-

CHUCK (V.O.)
(through walkie-talkie)
Rob, you're not gonna believe it but I'm getting all kinds (static).

ROB
Chuck. You broke up. Come back.

STATIC.

KAT
That's weird.

CHUCK (V.O.)
(through walkie-talkie)
Can you hear me now?

ROB
(into walkie-talkie)
Yes. Better.

CHUCK (V.O.)
(through walkie-talkie)
So I'm picking up crazy voices in the static. Hundreds of voices.

KEVIN
Did he say voices?

ROB
(into walkie-talkie)
Voices?

CHUCK (V.O.)
(through walkie-talkie)
(inaudible) (inaudible) (inaudible)

STATIC.

KAT
I better go check this out. Remember, don't go in without me.

ROB
Like I said, hurry up.

She cautiously heads down the hallway toward the staircase. Kevin primps again in the mirror. It cracks. He jumps back.

EXT. CAMP NAHGANO CAMPSITE - VAN - DUSK - SAME

The van violently JERKS and ROCKS as Chuck SCREAMS in pain.

INT. LODGE - FIRST FLOOR - AT THE SAME TIME

Samantha and Julie are back in the main room using the SPIRIT BOX. The pulsating loud static sound intermittently produces a clear word in a monotone MALE voice. Julie, still covered in greasy dust is now smeared from trying to remove it.

SPIRIT BOX
PASS (static) HOME (static) BURY

JULIE
Whose buried?

SPIRIT BOX
INNOCENT.

SAMANTHA
Who are you?

SPIRIT BOX
(static)

SAMANTHA
Hello?

SPIRIT BOX
(static)

JULIE
Whoa, that was cool. You think it was really something?

Tom stops filming.

TOM
Nah, it always just says random shit. Hey, let's set up the grid.

JULIE
Thought you said the spirit box was last. I need to wash this shit off.

TOM
You look fine.

JULIE
(sarcastic)
Seriously dude? Just give me a minute with Sam will ya?

TOM
Yeah sure.

Tom heads back over to the Buffalo head for a closer look as Julie approaches Samantha, speaks quietly.

JULIE
Hey, you wouldn't happen to have any tampons or napkins would you?

SAMANTHA
I do actually. They're in the van but I'm too lazy to go get 'em.

Kat comes bouncing down the stairway.

KAT
What are you too lazy to go get? I'm heading that way.
(MORE)

KAT (CONT'D)
Our batteries keep dying and Chuck's walkie isn't working.

SAMANTHA
I know, we tried calling him earlier. But hey, if you don't mind grab my tote bag. The green one?

KAT
Yeah sure (beat) Hey, Rob's about to open the only locked door up there. It might be good to get another angle from your camera.

TOM
Awesome. Sam, you coming?

JULIE
(toward Tom)
No, she's gonna help me find the little girls room. Aren't you?

Sam nods. Kat heads toward the exit.

KAT (O.C.)
I'll be back.

TOM
(toward Sam)
On second thought, I can assist you in any way you need.

SAMANTHA
(giggling)
No, I think we're good.

He heads up the stairs, turns back, smiles then resumes.

JULIE
(toward Sam)
Oooh gurl.

Samantha blushes.

EXT. CAMP NAHGANO LODGE - NIGHT

Kat comes bouncing out from the entrance into the chill of the night. The full moon illuminates everything including her breath. She pulls on her beanie and folds her arms, cold.

She heads toward the van taking in the beautiful night when out of the darkness an eagle swoops down dropping a feather that twirls and floats landing a few yards away from the van.

KAT
Okay, if that's not a sign.

She walks over to the feather, bends down just as the ground beneath her feet gives way, opens up, sucks her down. She's instantly gone. No sound. Only her beanie is left behind.

INT. LODGE - SECOND FLOOR

Rob waits at the door.

ROB
Where the hell is she?

TOM
Come on. Let's just do this. She can catch it on video.

ROB
Good point. Ready?

KEVIN
(into Tom's camera)
We're at the last room and of course it's locked. But Rob's got a tool for that.

Rob inserts a wire-like tool into the lock as Tom and Kevin stand back. A quick twist of the tool and CLICK, the door drifts open with a CREEEEK.

Rob kicks at the door, it swings all the way open revealing a web-covered dark and dusty control room with a panel of rusted levers, gears and switches. They enter.

ROB
What is this place?

KEVIN
Looks like some sort of control room. Is that a scoreboard?

Kevin wanders over to a dusty scoreboard marked 993. Rob bounces on the long bed. Dust billows.

ROB
Hey, check out this bed. Damn. Who ever slept here musta been tall.

Tom pans the camera. Kevin wanders to the window. Looks out.

TOM
Wonder what this room controlled.

INT. THE OTHER SIDE - CONTROL ROOM - SAME

The same exact room just looks clean and sterile. The Tall Man stands before the window, looking out. Ghostly apparitions of Rob, Kevin and Tom are seen walking about the room. The tall man turns as Kevin passes through him.

INT. LODGE - SECOND FLOOR - CONTROL ROOM - SAME

Startled, Kevin jolts forward.

KEVIN
Whoa, what was that?

TOM
What was what?

KEVIN
Freezing cold. It went right through me. Like ice!

TOM
Dude, you're by the window.

KEVIN
Thanks Captain obvious. It felt like someone walked right past.

ROB
No ones been here. Look, just our footprints are in the dust.

Kevin looks down. Sees a pair of large fresh shoe prints in front of the window. He GASPS.

KEVIN
Um, guys? What about these?

Tom and Rob walk over, look down.

ROB
I'll be damned. They look fresh.

Without warning, the shoe prints walk out of the room.

ROB (CONT'D)
(shocked)
Tell me you got that.

TOM
(satisfied)
Oh yeah.

KEVIN
(worried)
Check please.

INT. FIRST FLOOR HALLWAY

Sam and Julie walk the hallway shining their flashlights into rooms as they search.

JULIE
You'd think the damn bathroom would be off the main room but nooo.

SAMANTHA
I thought I saw it by the dining room earlier.

JULIE
And you didn't say anything?

SAMANTHA
I didn't have to go.

JULIE
No, you were distracted.

SAMANTHA
Distracted?

JULIE
Tom? He's totally hitting on you. So you and Rob broke up?

SAMANTHA
(firm)
That's *my* business.

JULIE
That's cool (beat) hey there it is!

The girls rush to a door marked GIRLS BATH AREA.

INT. BATH AREA

A once charming bath area now layered in dust and webs. The oval mirrors and sink basins, cracked and stained.

The girls enter and move into the room, their flashlights illuminate the peeling wallpaper and water-stained ceiling.

JULIE
Bingo. Let's see if we have water.

SAMANTHA
I highly doubt it.

There are three toilet stalls, all missing their doors and along the back, shower stalls with torn curtains. Samantha notices water in one of the toilets.

SAMANTHA (CONT'D)
I don't believe it. We have water.

A very happy Julie positions her flashlight onto the counter pointing toward the toilet stall.

JULIE
Where the hell is Kat? I need one of those things from your tote.

SAMANTHA
Damn her.

JULIE
Why don't you go get it. And get my purse too. I'm fine waiting here.

SAMANTHA
Are you sure? Because we can both-

JULIE
-No seriously. Go. Just hurry. Unless you gotta pee first.

SAMANTHA
No. I'm good. I'll be right back.

Sam leaves. Julie begins unbuckling her pants.

INT. LODGE - SECOND FLOOR

Tom continues filming as Rob speaks into his walkie-talkie. Kevin looks around the room, worried.

ROB
Come in base camp (pause) How we look'n? (pause) Yo Chuck! Kat! Where are you guys? We've got some serious sit going on up here.

Tom notices the footprints returning into the room, walking toward the scoreboard on the wall. Kevin holds his breath.

TOM
You guys seeing this?

Rob watches. Suddenly, the scoreboard changes from 993 to 994. Kevin turns, runs out.

EXT. CAMP NAHGANO - VAN - NIGHT - SAME

Samantha has made her way to the van. She slides open the door. Chuck sits with his back to her, headphones on. A half-smoked joint in the ashtray. The video monitors seem normal.

SAMANTHA
Hey, your walkie isn't working.

She digs for her tote. Finds it. Then grabs Julie's purse.

SAMANTHA (CONT'D)
Hey!

She grabs the back of his chair, spins him around. Her mouth drops. She falls backwards, screaming. CLOSE to see Chuck is a perfectly intact skeleton sitting upright in clothes.

INT. LODGE - FIRST FLOOR

Samantha comes screaming in just as Kevin runs down the staircase and SLAMS right into her. They collide, fall hard to the ground! Julie WALKS in.

JULIE
What the hell are you guys doing?

SAMANTHA
Those fuckers are pranking ME now.

JULIE
What the hell.

SAMANTHA
Come on Kevin, where'd he get that skeleton. Let me guess, Amazon?

KEVIN
What are you talking about?

SAMANTHA
Oh right, like you don't know.

Rob and Tom come barreling down the stairs, excited.

ROB
Did you hear what we got?

SAMANTHA
Oh, I heard alright *and* I saw it.

ROB
(excited)
You did?

TOM
That's awesome.

SAMANTHA
(toward Tom)
Whose side are you on?

Tom looks over at Rob, confused. Sam grabs her tote bag.

SAMANTHA (CONT'D)
And where the hell is Kat? Come on Julie, let's go wash up.

She snatches up the bags, heads toward the bath area.

Kevin gathers his stuff by the fireplace. He glances up at the Buffalo, it WINKS. He runs.

A disembodied BELLY-LAUGH reverberates throughout the room. Rob and Tom run like hell, follow Kevin out the door.

EXT. CAMP NAHGANO ENTRANCE - NIGHT

Rob, Tom and Kevin come barreling out heading toward the van.

KEVIN
What the fuck was that?

TOM
That was bizarre.

ROB
Oh my God that crazy laugh. Fuck. Hope we got that on the recorders.

KEVIN
That fucking buffalo winked at me.

Rob and Tom LAUGH.

TOM
Paranormal attraction dude.

KEVIN
Fuck you.

ROB
But Kev, look at the bright side, we actually just caught a real-

KEVIN
(toward Rob)
-Go ahead. Laugh it up. I hate you.

They LAUGH.

ROB
But you lived to tell about it. Now watch, Julie and Sam will come running out any second.

They turn, look toward the lodge, wait.

INT. BATH AREA

Sam is waiting by the sink, Julie comes out of the stall.

JULIE
You're a lifesaver.

SAMANTHA
No biggie. Just wish I'd start.

JULIE
Are you late?

SAMANTHA
God, I hope not.

JULIE
Dare I ask who? Never mind. Not my business. But, if you want a test I have a couple extra in my bag.

Samantha's eyes wide, surprised.

SAMANTHA
You have pregnancy tests?

JULIE
I was late with my ex. Thank God it was negative. But I bought a whole box and never took 'em out. You know. Lazy. You should take one. Peace of mind.

Julie reaches into her purse to grab one.

SAMANTHA
No, thanks. I don't need it.

Julie pulls her hand back from the purse.

JULIE
Okay, suit yourself.

Julie drops her purse next to the sink then positions her flashlight onto the counter pointing toward the shower.

Julie attempts to turn the faucet, it's tight.

JULIE (CONT'D)
Come on, help me.

SAMANTHA
What, you gonna take a shower? Just wash up in the sink.

JULIE
Have you seen the sinks?

Sam notices all the sinks are cracked and faucets broken.

SAMANTHA
What about the kitchen?

Julie continues trying to turn the water handle. It's stuck.

JULIE
I'm already here. And If I get this son of a bitch to work and water comes out, I'm showering. You can get me clean clothes, right?

SAMANTHA
If this thing works, I'll get you clean clothes and a towel.

JULIE
(laughing)
You *better* get me a towel.

The girls attempt to turn the handle but it's corroded.

SAMANTHA
We need a wrench.

JULIE
Then go grab one. I'll keep trying.

SAMANTHA
Leave you here. Again?

JULIE
Come on. You already did it once and I survived.

SAMANTHA
Okay brave one. I'll be right back.

Samantha exits the bath area just as Julie successfully turns the handle. Water flows. It looks clear, clean.

JULIE
(yelling)
Hey Sam! I got it! It's good!

She holds her hand in the water.

JULIE (CONT'D)
It's warm even!

She starts removing her clothes.

JULIE (CONT'D)
(yelling)
Sam! Did you hear me? I got it!

INT. LODGE - FIRST FLOOR

Samantha has just left the bath area but doesn't hear Julie. She shines her flashlight toward the grand room up ahead until the sound of a pan hitting the ground in the kitchen is heard.

SAMANTHA
Hello?

A distant VOICE sounding a lot like Tom is heard.

VOICE-TOM
Hey Sam.

SAMANTHA
Tom?

She maneuvers toward the kitchen, curious.

SAMANTHA (CONT'D)
Tom? Where are you?

She continues into the dark kitchen.

EXT. CAMP NAHGANO CAMPSITE - VAN - NIGHT

The guys turn away from the lodge, head toward the van.

ROB
Guess they're not coming.

TOM
I should go back. Just in case.

ROB
Sam can handle herself. I'm surprised you don't know that.

TOM
I know she's a strong woman.

Rob approaches Tom. Kevin takes the cue, keeps walking.

ROB
Look, Samantha and I have been together six years. Six.

TOM
But she said you guys broke up and after Tehachapi, she's moving on.

ROB
Yep, just like she said after San Diego. And then after Denver and Tucson. But you know, this time I'm done with the drama. Just show me a little respect.

Rob turns, follows Kevin toward the van.

INT. BATH AREA

Julie's dirty clothes are draped over the stall. Her flashlight perched on the sink as the shower water flows.

EXT. CAMP NAHGANO CAMPSITE - VAN - NIGHT

They all walk up to the van, stop dead in their tracks.

ROB
Is this a joke?

They see a skeleton in Chuck's clothes. Tom LAUGHS.

TOM
Good one. Must be why Sam got so pissed off.

ROB
You think? Okay Chuck. You can come out now. Ha ha, very funny.

KEVIN
Yo Chuck, this is classic man.

TOM
Hope you got it on film. Damn, I woulda loved to have seen her face.

Rob throws Tom a frown.

ROB
Come on little bro. You made her scream. Now let's wrap this up.

They all wait. Nothing.

ROB (CONT'D)
Where the hell is he? Chuck!

Rob climbs into the van. As he does, he notices the spare batteries still in the box.

ROB (CONT'D)
The spare batteries are still in here. Kat never got 'em.

KEVIN
Probably scared her off like Sam.

ROB
Then why didn't she come back in?

Tom moves in close to the skeleton.

TOM
Damn, this is a really good quality prop. Looks real.

KEVIN
When have you ever seen a real one.

TOM
I saw that deer.

ROB
I mean, why would he do this?

KEVIN
Why would he do this? Rob, he's the prankster of all pranksters.

ROB
But go to all this trouble for what? And where did he keep it?

TOM
Where the spare shoulda been?

KEVIN
What a slob!

Referring to all the white tissues strewn about.

ROB
Yep, classic Chuck. Okay, jokes over. CHUCK! YO! Let's go!

Nothing. Kevin sees something on the ground a few yards away.

KEVIN
Hey, something's over here.

He jogs over, picks it up. Holds it up.

KEVIN (CONT'D)
It's Kat's beanie!

ROB
Like they wanted us to find it.

TOM
So they're both pranking us.

KEVIN
I bet they're watching right now.

Kevin jogs back, looks around.

KEVIN (CONT'D)
Laughing at us. Am I right?

No response. Samantha hurriedly approaches.

SAMANTHA
So, everyone had a good laugh on my expense I'm sure?

KEVIN
On all our expenses, actually.

SAMANTHA
What's that supposed to mean?

KEVIN
Chuck's skeleton joke and now we find Kat's beanie on the ground. We think they're both pranking us.

SAMANTHA
Well that's a bunch of shit. Why would Kat even do that. Stupid.
(yelling)
Yeah I said it, stupid prank!
(toward Tom)
And what the fuck. I hear you in the kitchen then you're out here?

TOM
I've been here all along.

SAMANTHA
Whatever. Look, I need a wrench to fix a faucet.

ROB
What faucet?

SAMANTHA
The one in the bathroom shower, Julie's trying to get it to work.

KEVIN
Oh my God, you left her in there?

ROB
By herself?

JULIE
She was fine.

ROB
You didn't hear that voice?

KEVIN
The crazy ass voice?

TOM
It mighta been Chuck.

ROB
That wasn't Chuck.

Kevin agrees.

SAMANTHA
(toward Tom)
Only voice I heard was yours, but you say it wasn't you.

TOM
It wasn't.

ROB
(excited)
Sam, think we caught a *real* ghost.

TOM
Allegedly. I need to be convinced.

SAMANTHA
Oh my God, you're gonna start in with that again?

KEVIN
He's not shit'n you this time. I mean, we saw it.

SAMANTHA
(not convinced)
You saw it?

TOM
It *was* compelling.

SAMANTHA
You're not fucking with me?

All three of the guys respond in unison, NOPE. Sam becomes worried.

SAMANTHA (CONT'D)
Holy shit. Julie.

KEVIN
Um, I'm not going back in there.

SAMANTHA
Fine. You big wuss.

TOM
Well I have to. My camera's still in there.

ROB
All our equipment's in there.

TOM
Look, I'll go grab our stuff. It'll give me another chance to debunk that voice and those footprints.

ROB
Okay, why don't Kevin and I search for Chuck and Kat. You both go get Julie. Grab whatever gear you can and let's get the fuck outta here.

KEVIN
Thank you for not making me go.

SAMANTHA
Footprints?

TOM
I'll tell you on the way.

Samantha grabs a wrench and Julie's bag.

EXT. CAMP NAHGANO - VAN- NIGHT

Rob's flashlight shines near where Kevin found the beanie.

ROB
KAAAATTTT! CHUCCCKKK!

Kevin climbs up on the bumper of the van.

KEVIN
Yo CHUCK! KAAATTT!

Kevin looks around the moon lit area, sees something, points.

KEVIN (CONT'D)
Hey. Over there! A dome tent. Just over the tops of the trees.

ROB
Maybe they know something.

Kevin jumps down.

INT. CAVE - SAME

Kat lay unconscious on the floor of a small cave. It's dark, cold and damp. A steady DRIP of water is heard. The only light, the glow from her wolf fang necklace around her neck tucked into her shirt. The eagle feather lay nearby.

The wolfdog sits next to her, waiting.

EXT. BATH AREA

Sam and Tom arrive at the bath area door.

SAMANTHA
Stay here, I'll go give her the towel and stuff. And don't say anything about the, you know. She might freak.

TOM
Look, you get her and I'll go grab our stuff. Meet you at the van.

SAMANTHA
That means going upstairs. Alone. And you're not scared?

TOM
Not if you're waiting for me.

She fake smiles. He turns, shines his flashlight forward.

INT. BATH AREA

Samantha comes through the door, Julie's flashlight flickers. We HEAR the water still flowing.

SAMANTHA
(loud)
Can't believe you got it running.

No answer.

SAMANTHA (CONT'D)
Did you hear me? I have your towel.

JULIE (O.C.)
You already gave me a towel.

SAMANTHA
No I didn't.

Sam looks around, uneasy, then notices Julie's purse, reaches inside, searching. She pulls out an extra pregnancy test.

SAMANTHA (CONT'D)
Hey, I'm taking one of the tests!

JULIE (O.C.)
What?

SAMANTHA
Just hurry up will ya?

Sam ducks into a toilet stall. The SHOWER continues.

INT. CAVE - SAME

The glowing necklace seems brighter. The small cave interior more visible. Wolfdog licks at Kat's face. She stirs then wakes. Opens her eyes, jolts backwards at the sight of wolfdog who immediately sits up, raises a paw, friendly.

KAT
(hesitant)
Are you a nice doggy?

Hesitating, she reaches out, shakes his paw. He licks her.

KAT (CONT'D)
Well hello there.

She releases his paw. He sits down with his front paws outstretched like an Egyptian Sphinx. She pats his head.

KAT (CONT'D)
How the heck did we get in here?

She looks around then notices the glow from the necklace under her shirt.

KAT (V.O.)
Whoa. This is new.

She pulls the necklace up, it glows bright yellow illuminating everything! She looks around then stands, circles the small space, realizing there's no way out.

KAT
Where the hell are we?

She instantly shivers from the cold. The wolfdog whimpers. A wisp of wind whips through the small chamber.

KAT (CONT'D)
What was that?

The wolfdog moves to the opposite wall, sits and whimpers. Kat approaches, holds up her glowing necklace to view the wall when she notices a small indented shape in the stone. She moves in to see an exact shape of her wolf fang necklace.

KAT (V.O.)
No. Can't be.

She holds it up to the indented shape. A perfect match.

KAT
Okay, that's weird.

She looks down at wolfdog for approval. He loudly BARKS. The SOUND reverberates throughout. Kat covers her ears.

KAT (CONT'D)
No barking.

He whimpers and sits down. She slowly snaps the fang into the indent CLICK. A HISS and CRUNCH as a stone wall rolls aside revealing another larger dark space.

Kat moves slowly toward the dark opening, her necklace illuminating the way, wolfdog by her side, they enter.

EXT. CAMP NAHGANO - NIGHT

Rob and Kevin come upon the dome tent illuminated by the full moon. The campfire outside still smolders. As they approach, they see pant legs and shoes sticking out.

KEVIN
Looks like someone's inside.

Kevin approaches. Rob follows.

KEVIN (CONT'D)
Hello? Excuse me?

They arrive at the entrance. Kevin looks in. He stumbles backwards, GASPING. Rob approaches.

ROB
What's wrong?

INT. LODGE - SECOND FLOOR - SAME

Tom has an arm full of I.R Cameras, voice recorders and his camera slung around his neck. He makes his way along the hallway toward the last I.R camera next to the control room.

He nears the room, side-glances inside to see the 994 on the scoreboard. The door SLAMS shut. He jumps back. Quickly reaches for the last I.R Camera when dozens of wallpaper hands protrude from the wallpaper, grabbing, pulling at him.

He sees his reflection in the mirror as the hands rip and tear at his clothes and skin, pulling him apart before his eyes, He SCREAMS in pain before being pulled through. The equipment drops to the floor, the camera still filming.

The control room door slowly opens. The scoreboard reads 995.

EXT. DOME TENT - NIGHT - A MOMENT LATER

Rob and Kevin stand outside the dome tent peering inside to see a fully dressed Native American man, flat on his back. Only he's a pure-white skeleton. His mouth agape in a scream.

KEVIN
Jesus. Another one. What is it with this place and skeletons?

Rob crouches down next to the smoldering campfire.

ROB
The coals are still warm.

KEVIN
This is a set up, am I right?

ROB
You would think so.

Rob checks the pockets for identification, finds a cellphone.

ROB (CONT'D)
Huh, the new one, just came out.

KEVIN
So there you go. For sure a prank.

Rob presses the button. The phone lights up.

ROB
It has juice.

Rob lifts the cellphone high into the air.

KEVIN
Any bars?

ROB
Nope.

KEVIN
Hey look. It's Kat's fang necklace.

Kevin bends down, snatches up the necklace and pockets it.

KEVIN (CONT'D)
(loud)
Funny! Ha Ha guys! Nice touch!

Rob looks closer at the skeleton. A sudden urgency grabs him.

ROB
We need to get back to the van.

KEVIN
But what about Chuck and Kat?

ROB
They're not out here.

Kevin looks at the skeleton then back at Rob. His eyes widen. They quickly head back through the brush and trees.

INT. BATH AREA

Samantha leans against the peeling wall of the toilet stall holding the pregnancy test in her hand, hesitant to try. The shower water SOUND continues in the background.

KAT
Hey, hurry up will ya?

INT. CAVE - SAME

Kat and wolfdog are now in a larger chamber. Native American paintings cover the walls and ceiling. She walks along, illuminating the drawings with the light of the wolf fang.

KAT
It's a story about these people.

She lightly drags her fingers along the painted images.

KAT (CONT'D)
Life was wonderful, prosperous.

Her finger stops at an image of an enchanted wolf with glowing fangs descending from the sky, welcomed by all.

KAT (CONT'D)
Look, a wolfdog like you. And look, its fangs, they're glowing.

She holds up her wolf fang necklace, curious. Then continues walking along the wall to the next drawing that depicts many moons of good fortune. A flock of black birds drop seeds to plant as the Native people harvest. A mother holds a baby.

KAT (CONT'D)
The wolf was a protector, the birds helpful for many moons. But then-

In the next image, the wolf's glowing fangs have disappeared and the enchanted wolf ascends upward into a burst of stars.

KAT (CONT'D)
Whoa. Could it be?

She pulls her wolf fang necklace up again, compares it to the image. Wolfdog whimpers. She continues along the wall.

KAT (CONT'D)
An evil presence brought death.

She illuminates the second-to-last drawing that depicts the storm Gods attempt to stop the evil entity. Another failure.

KAT (CONT'D)
Death and destruction.
(toward wolfdog)
It was terrible.

Wolfdog whimpers. A shiver runs down her spine. BURRRR.

POOF! A small fire instantly appears inside a fire pit.

She stumbles backwards, trips over a thick fur folded on the ground. She snatches it up, wraps it around her, warmth. She backs away from the fire, cautious. The flames flicker.

EXT. THE OTHER SIDE - GARDENS - DAY

Chuck appears disoriented as he wanders through a beautifully manicured maze-like garden. He comes upon the back-side of Halbert who peeks through the bushes toward the lodge.

CHUCK
Hey man, can you help me?

Halbert whips around, nervous. He crouches down.

HALBERT
What are you doing here?

CHUCK
Have you seen my friends?

HALBERT
Shh. I can't be talking to you.

CHUCK
Why? What is this place?

Halbert exhales a deep SIGH but continues crouching.

HALBERT
If he sees me talking to you-

CHUCK
-Who? Who are you afraid of?

Chuck crouches down as well.

HALBERT
My boss. He's pure evil.

CHUCK
Must be a real asshole.

HALBERT
You have no idea.

Halbert looks around, cautious.

HALBERT (CONT'D)
(sighs)
Oh what does it matter. It's almost over anyway.

CHUCK
What's almost over?

HALBERT
Look, this may be hard to accept but my boss has been collecting souls over two centuries.

CHUCK
Old dude with a shoe fetish?

HALBERT
Not that kind of sole. Your soul.

CHUCK
Well he's not getting mine.

HALBERT
He already did.

Chuck drops his jaw, shocked.

HALBERT (CONT'D)
Look, he completely decimated the Tribe that once lived on this land.
(MORE)

HALBERT (CONT'D)
And then anyone who came upon it, like you did. When he reaches one thousand, he gains ultimate power.

CHUCK
What are you saying?

HALBERT
Once your friends arrive. It's all over. I'm sorry, we can't stop him.

Chuck looks around worried.

INT. BATH AREA

Samantha exits the toilet stall just as the SQUEAK of the faucet is heard. The water stops. Julie, still in the stall, dries herself off. Sam realizes she's holding the test strip. Shakes it twice then quickly stuffs it into her pocket.

SAMANTHA
Jesus. Longest shower ever.

JULIE (O.S.)
I'm not pay'n the water bills. It was funny, as soon as you left I got it working. I yelled at you.

SAMANTHA
Well I didn't hear you.

JULIE (O.S.)
And it was warm.

Julie steps from the shower stall, towel wrapped around her. She's covered head to toe in blood. Samantha jumps back.

SAMANTHA
What the fuck?!

JULIE
(confused)
What.

SAMANTHA
What do you mean what, you're covered in blood!

Julie looks down at herself. From her POV she's fine.

JULIE (O.C.)
What are you talking about?

Julie turns, sees herself in the cracked mirror. To her horror she sees herself covered in blood. She SCREAMS.

She runs past Sam, pushes the door open and continues running toward the grand room, leaving bloody footprints as she goes. Sam barrels out the bathroom door after her.

SAMANTHA
Julie! Wait!

INT. OTHERSIDE - CONTROL ROOM - SAME

It's the same large bright room with wall-mounted monitors and controls. The tall man, watches the monitor as he doubles over in LAUGHTER. It reverberates throughout the room.

EXT. CAMP NAHGANO - LODGE ENTRANCE - SAME

At the threshold of the doorway, scores of ants are barely held back by the powdery substance spread across the opening.

EXT. CAMP NAHGANO - ENTRANCE - VAN

Julie comes running out leaving behind bloody footprints and crying hysterically. The ants take notice and quickly follow consuming the bloody footprints. She trips, falls. The ants quickly eat their way toward her. She gets up, runs again.

SAMANTHA (O.S.)
JULIE! Wait up!

Sam gets to the van just as Julie drops next to it, crying.

SAMANTHA (CONT'D)
I'm getting water!

JULIE
(crying)
What the fuck is this!

Sam rushes around back to grab the water when Rob and Kevin run up. Rob notices the disappearing bloody footprints. He sees the ants are approaching fast and almost upon her.

ROB
Look out! Ants!

Julie sees the approaching ants, SCREAMS.

Sam comes around with containers of water. She tosses one to Rob as she pops the cap, a CRACK of thunder and the clouds open up releasing torrents of rain instantly washing away the blood and ants. Sam throws a clean towel on Julie who WEEPS.

INT. OTHERSIDE - CONTROL ROOM - SAME

The tall man becomes instantly mad as he SLAMS his fists on the table BAM! The scoreboard still reads: 995.

INT. VAN - SAME

Everyone quickly rushes inside the van, awkwardly away from the skeleton. Julie sobs as Sam grabs clean clothes.

JULIE
Oh my God! What the fuck. Did you see those ants chasing me?

SAMANTHA
Good thing for that downpour!

KEVIN
Did that shit come outta the faucet? Was it like blood?

ROB
Could be paranormal.

KEVIN
Like being slimed? And those ants. Never seen anything like it. Ever.

ROB
Me neither.

Julie whimpers as Sam holds up a sheet to block her dressing.

SAMANTHA
(looking around)
Where's Tom?

ROB
Thought he was with you.

SAMANTHA
He was getting our stuff. Said he'd meet here back at the van.

KEVIN
Great. Now you left Tom in there?

ROB
He's a big boy.

SAMANTHA
What's that supposed to mean?

ROB
I think you know.

Julie whips the sheet away, now dressed in shorts and a top.

JULIE
Can we please get outta here?!
(toward the skeleton)
And what the hell is that?

SAMANTHA
Chuck's stupid prank.

JULIE
So where is he and where's Kat?

ROB
We don't know.

JULIE
What do you mean you don't know.

SAMANTHA
And you haven't seen Tom?

ROB
Haven't seen any of 'em.

KEVIN
(toward the skeleton)
Or have we?

SAMANTHA
What's that supposed to mean?

KEVIN
(toward Rob)
Look, you saw the guy in the tent.

SAMANTHA
What guy?

JULIE
What tent?

KEVIN
And the ants almost attack Julie.

JULIE
That was horrifying.

KEVIN
I don't think it's a prank.

SAMANTHA
Can someone please speak English?

ROB
Look, I see where you're going but it just isn't possible. I mean, if this isn't a prank like you say, which I doubt, then this'll have a chipped tooth, which it won't-

Rob swivels the chair to reveal the skeleton's chipped tooth. Startled he GASPS and jolts backwards.

SAMANTHA
That doesn't mean anything Rob. You know more than anyone here that Chuck's a perfectionist. We've all seen his perfect pranks. This is no different.

ROB
But would he be enough of a perfectionist to put a screw in the shoulder from a childhood accident?

SAMANTHA
Probably not.

Rob pulls down the shirt covering the shoulder to reveal a shiny stainless steel screw holding the bones together. He quickly stumbles from the van into the rain. They follow.

ROB
Holy shit. What the fuck?

The rain suddenly stops. The clouds part revealing a full moon illuminating everything. Julie hesitates, then steps from the van. Rob collapses to his knees, distraught.

JULIE
What just happened?

SAMANTHA
None of this makes any sense. How could that be him. From Chuck to that? In an hour? No way.

JULIE
(pointing to the van)
You think that's Chuck?

SAMANTHA
They're still pranking us.

ROB
Do I look like I'm pranking?

SAMANTHA
Then how can you say this.

KEVIN
Don't you see the tissues?

SAMANTHA
What about 'em.

KEVIN
They're all over the place.

SAMANTHA
Yeah, typical for when he has a-

KEVIN
Bloody nose.

ROB
Bloody nose.

ROB (CONT'D)
(realization)
He had a fucking bloody nose.

JULIE
There's no blood on the tissues.

ROB
Exactly.

Rob turns away, distraught.

KEVIN
Remember Rob's sandwich? The paper towel? None of us copped to it because none of us did it. The deer, the lens stuck in it's eye. The sandwich, don't you see?

JULIE
What are you saying?

Rob wipes his tear-filled face.

ROB
That when I hit the deer something ate it to the bone just like it ate my sandwich and cleaned the paper towel. It's attracted to blood.

JULIE
Oh my God they were gonna eat me?!

She jumps back in the van.

KEVIN
You know the van didn't save him.

She jumps back out again.

ROB
Oh my God, this can't be happening. Just grab what we can and let's get the fuck outta here. Leave the tents, I don't care. Let's just go.

KEVIN
But what about Kat and Tom? The equipment inside?

ROB
You wanna go back in there?

KEVIN
Hell no.

They pile back in the van.

KEVIN (CONT'D)
What about - - Chuck back there.

ROB
I'm not leaving him here.

Julie slides further from Chuck's skeleton.

JULIE
You sure about that?

Rob turns the key VROOOM.

EXT. CAMP NAHGANO - CAMPSITE - VAN

As soon as he puts it into gear and hits the gas, the back tires spin in the muddy ground from the recent downpour. He tries a few times before Kevin, Sam and Julie jump out.

KEVIN
Find anything to give it traction.

They fan out. Kevin finds a few sticks, tosses them in front of the tire for traction. Sam notices blood on Julie's shorts.

SAMANTHA
Oh my God, Julie. Your shorts.

Julie looks down.

JULIE
Oh shit. Fucking period.

She rushes back toward the van when she notices movement on the ground coming toward her. Ants burst through the bushes.

JULIE (CONT'D)
Ants!

The ants rush toward Julie at lightning speed.

JULIE (CONT'D)
Oh my God!

She turns, runs straight for the cliff and rushing river twenty feet below. The ants are at her heels as she leaps.

SLOW as she falls toward the water. The ants devouring her feet and legs to the bone as she drops. SPLASH.

She flails around as the current takes her down river, SCREAMING for help as she goes.

JULIE (CONT'D)
HELLLLPPPP!

EXT./INT. VAN - A MOMENT LATER

Shocked, Kevin jumps back inside the van.

KEVIN
Hurry! Go! Go! Follow the river!

SAMANTHA
I'm not leaving Tom here!

ROB
No time to debate.

Samantha hesitates, then backs away from the van. Rob flashes her a disappointed look, then throws it into gear.

KEVIN
Go! Go!

The van quickly pulls away. Samantha watches them go.

EXT. CAMP NAHGANO - CAMPSITE - ROAD

The van veers off onto a dirt road that parallels the river kicking up dust. Gaining ground, the van catches up with Julie who clings to something as she flails in the water.

The horn HONKS signaling they're coming.

INT. CONTROL ROOM

The tall man, now transfixed on the monitor, watches the van race along the dirt road parallel to the river. He waves his hand over one of the many buttons on the control panel.

TALL MAN
Oops.

EXT. ROAD - SAME

The van races, gaining ground when without warning, a tree up ahead falls directly across the road. BAM!

INT. VAN

The tree SMASHES across the road. Rob hits the brakes.

ROB
Shit!

EXT. ROAD - SAME

The van slides to a stop. The van doors open, Rob and Kevin jump out and muscle the branch away from the path.

ROB (O.C.)
Good enough!

Rob and Kevin jump back in and the van peels away.

EXT. CAMP NAHGANO CAMPSITE - AT THE SAME TIME

Sam stands near the lodge, looks up, sees the curtains move.

SAMANTHA
I knew you were in there.
(yelling)
Tom! Come on! Hurry up!

Black birds begin to gather in the trees. Sam doesn't notice.

EXT. VAN

The van, once again parallels the river. Moving faster they catch up to Julie who somehow stays above water.

INT. VAN

Kevin points out his window.

KEVIN
There she is! She's right there.

Rob begins honking the horn again. HONK, HONK-HONK!

KEVIN (CONT'D)
Faster, gotta get ahead of her.

Rob floors the gas peddle. Dust billows behind them.

EXT. CAMP NAHGANO - CAMPSITE

Hundreds of black birds have settled upon anything and everything. Sam looks around, notices.

SAMANTHA (V.O.)
Alfred Hitchcock much?

She starts to yell for Tom but realizes that's not a good idea and instead slowly heads toward the lodge entrance when all at once the birds swoop down toward her as if keeping her away from and entering the lodge.

She turns, runs as fast as she can back to the tent, zips herself inside. The birds swoop and gather outside her tent.

INT. TENT

Out of breath, Sam frantically looks around for something to protect her from the birds outside. She grabs and begins putting on extra jackets when she remembers the test strip in her pocket. She hesitates a moment, then pulls it out to see.

EXT. CAMP NAHGANO - RIVERBANK

The van slides to a stop. Rob and Kevin jump out, rush toward the riverbank.

KEVIN
I see her!

Kevin rushes into the fast-moving river going from boulder to boulder to intercept Julie. Rob is close behind.

Julie comes barreling toward him fast, head above water.

ROB
Grab her! Grab her!

Kevin reaches out, grabs Julie's arm swinging her from the current. Rob jumps in helps pull her. Dragging her out.

She's very dead and white as a ghost. Her legs and feet are nothing but bone. Rob and Kevin fall backwards.

KEVIN
Holy shit.

ROB
What the fuck?

KEVIN
Oh my God dude, she bled out.

Rob turns away from the horrifying scene.

At that moment, a huge tree limb breaks, falls from the tree above, bashing Kevin in the face. He falls to the ground.

Rob jumps back.

ROB
What the fuck? Kevin!

Rob rushes to his side but quickly realizes there's nothing he can do. CLOSE on the horror that's Kevin's face. Bashed in and partially missing with brain matter exposed.

Rob covers his mouth as he gags. Stumbles backwards.

From out of the fallen tree limb come hundreds of bees swarming. Rob leaps inside the van, slams the door.

INT. VAN

Rob skillfully swats the few bees who made it inside. SMACK!

EXT. CAMP NAHGANO - SOMEWHERE - SAME

Another cone-shaped anthill that seems quiet and dormant suddenly comes to life as ants burst from the spout in a lava flow of ants heading along the riverbank toward Kevin's body.

INT. CAVE

Kat kneels close to the fire, briskly rubbing her hands together when the flames turn bluish-orange and the silhouette of a GREAT CHIEF materializes. Shocked, she stumbles backwards.

GREAT CHIEF (V.O.)
Katrina, daughter of Soaring Eagle and the last of our people. You've been summoned by the great Gods.

She rubs her head, looks over at wolfdog.

KAT
Whoa, I musta *really* hit my head.

The flames intensify. She falls to the ground.

KAT (CONT'D)
Okay, you have my attention.

GREAT CHIEF (V.O.)
Three thousand full moons ago, an evil engulfed our land, enslaving our people, collecting their souls. Every attempt to stop this has failed. Even our greatest Gods have been no match for this evil bind.

KAT
Like the drawings. On the wall.

GREAT CHIEF (V.O.)
But the recent awakening of the enchanted fang has given new hope. Only two in existence, together their power greater than any God. But the Brave who carried the other, has been lost.

Kat holds up the leather corded fang around her neck.

GREAT CHIEF (V.O.)
You Katrina, are our last hope.

KAT
Whoa. I'm not sure I can do anything. I mean, I don't know-

GREAT CHIEF (V.O.)
-There is no time! To save our people and your friends you must repeat my words, exactly.

KAT
My friends are they okay? Are they safe?

The flames intensify even greater.

KAT (CONT'D)
Okay. I'm sorry, I will. But I need to know one thing.

The flames flicker.

KAT (CONT'D)
If you're saying I'm full Kawaiisu, then please, who was my father? Please I need to know.

GREAT CHIEF (V.O.)
He will be revealed soon enough but first you must light the sage, raise the feather. Repeat my words.

His likeness dissipates into the flames. His voice echos.

GREAT CHIEF (V.O.)
Omis hilis haya Hentha.

KAT
Omis hilis haya Heniha.

She holds the sage smudge-stick to the fire, lights it.

GREAT CHIEF (V.O.)
Taka Hechee sokhe mado.

KAT
Taka Hechee sokhe mado.

She raises the eagle feather upward.

GREAT CHIEF (V.O.)
An Nuwu!

KAT
An Nuwu!

The outlines of indigenous people appear as moving light patterns on the walls and ceiling. A low drum beat begins. The images dance to the beat as she summons past leaders.

The wolf fang around her neck glows even brighter.

EXT. CAMP NAHGANO RIVERBANK - SAME

Kevin's lifeless body lay just beyond the riverbank. The wolf fang necklace in his pocket begins to glow BLUE just as the ants arrive. The ants closest to his body incinerate into a circle of dead ants, the other ants quickly retreat.

The blue-glowing fang becomes brighter and brighter.

EXT. CAMP NAHGANO ROAD - LODGE ENTRANCE - DAY

The van zooms along the road toward the lodge entrance kicking up dust. It heads straight to where Sam had been. As the van slides to a stop it forces a cluster of black birds from around the tent to take flight.

INT. VAN

Rob peers out the dusty window to see Samantha burst from the tent. She rushes to the van, limping.

SAMANTHA (O.C.)
Open the door! Open the door!

Rob jumps from his seat unlocks, pushes open the passenger door. She jumps in, frantic. She slams the door.

SAMANTHA (CONT'D)
Go go!

He throws it into drive, whips a u-turn as they barrel away from the lodge.

ROB
No Tom?

SAMANTHA
No. I saw a curtain move upstairs
but then those birds attacked me.

ROB
Are you okay?

SAMANTHA
I'm fine. What's with all these
dead bees?

She whips around looking for Julie and Kevin.

SAMANTHA (CONT'D)
Where's Kevin? And Julie?

ROB
They didn't make it.

SAMANTHA
What?!

The van drives fast, heading toward that narrow-road section when Rob notices two shadowy figures up ahead in the road.

ROB
Who's that?

He leans forward. Samantha turns to look.

EXT. CAMP NAHGANO ROAD - AT THE SAME TIME

Two shadowy FIGURES illuminated by the full moon, slowly walk the center of the road toward the approaching van.

INT. VAN

Now almost upon them-

Rob's POV to see it's Kevin and Julie. Both pale. Kevin with his bashed in and partially missing face and Julie with her stark-white skin, skeleton legs and feet.

Samantha GASPS. Rob swerves. They plow into a tree. CRASH!

EXT. CAMP NAHGANO ROAD

Smoke billows from the front of the van, now partially wrapped around the tree. Periodic sparks and dripping gas.

INT. VAN

Rob MOANS as he slowly swivels his head toward Sam but she's gone. The seat, empty. The windshield, missing. He unbuckles, pulls himself from the seat. Excruciating pain from a metal rod in his thigh. He tries removing it but can't.

He turns to see Chuck's skeleton now without a head. He attempts to open the driver door, it's stuck.

ROB
Sam! Sam!

He maneuvers to the passenger seat door. Grabs the handle and pushes with all his strength, it opens. He falls onto the ground. PAIN! He instantly throws up.

He begins crawling toward the front of the van, searching.

ROB (CONT'D)
Sam? Samantha?!

No response. He tries to stand but his injured leg forces him back to the ground. He continues crawling, slithering.

EXT. CAMP NAHGANO - THE OTHER SIDE - DAY

The tall grass sways in the gentle breeze. Birds sing. Samantha lifts her head. She instantly sits up, looks around.

SAMANTHA
Rob!

She looks down at herself and realizes she's no longer injured. Her clothes, clean. She touches her belly. Confused, she stands. Instantly notices the large tree with the crashed van. Moving closer, she sees the van, smoking and sparking.

SAMANTHA (CONT'D)
Rob?

The van ignites into a ball of fire. Engulfing the front.

She sees Rob. He's injured and bleeding, crawling toward something on the ground. She rushes to him but instantly hits an invisible barrier dividing them. She can't get through. She pounds on it but nothing happens, not even a sound.

SAMANTHA (CONT'D)
Rob! Can you hear me? I'm here!

He doesn't hear her and continues crawling toward something.

EXT. CAMP NAHGANO ROAD - TREE - AT THE SAME TIME

Rob has made his way to the twisted body of Samantha.

ROB
Oh no, no, no.

He scoots closer to her, cradles her lifeless head in his arms, he checks for a pulse. He begins to rock her and cry.

ROB (CONT'D)
Sam no! Please don't die. Please.

EXT. CAMP NAHGANO - THE OTHER SIDE

Samantha, now standing against the invisible barrier whimpers as she watches Rob cradling someone that looks like - - wait, it's her! Her mouth drops in disbelief and shock.

SAMANTHA
Rob, I'm here. Can't you see me? Can't you hear me? I can hear you!

ROB
(from the other side)
Sam I shoulda told you this sooner.

SAMANTHA
Told me what? Tell me.

ROB
(from the other side)
You know you've always been the light of my life. My soul mate.

SAMANTHA
I feel the same way. I'm sorry I tried to make you jealous.

ROB
(from the other side)
I was always way too jealous. After San Diego, Denver, Tucson.

SAMANTHA
It was me! I was doing that. I don't know why. I'm sorry.

Rob lovingly brushes the hair from her forehead.

ROB
(from the other side)
So here I am, pouring out my heart to you once again and you can't even hear me. Typical. I guess it doesn't matter what I was gonna say. Might as well just say it.

He kisses her forehead.

SAMANTHA
I have something to say as well!

ROB
(from the other side)
I was leaving you.

SAMANTHA (CONT'D)
I'm pregnant.

SAMANTHA (CONT'D)
Leaving me? But you're the father!

KEVIN (O.S.)
Hey, there you are. We've been look'n all over for you.

JULIE (O.S.)
Who's a father?

Sam whips around to see Kevin, Tom and Julie looking better than normal. As if nothing has happened. They approach her.

KEVIN
Come on Sam, we gotta go.

Sam backs away.

SAMANTHA
Stay away from me. I saw you.
(toward Julie)
And you. Both dead. Way dead.

TOM
What are you talking about? They're right here.

JULIE
Yeah Sam, I'm right here.

SAMANTHA
(toward Tom)
And you. I don't know how you died but you're dead too. I know it.

TOM
I don't feel dead.

A TALL MAN with a wide gaping smile arrives.

TALL MAN
Ahh, there you are. Our newest members. Tom, Kevin, Julie and Samantha, although you sometimes go by Sam. May I call you Sam?

SAMANTHA
Who are you and why are we here?

TALL MAN
Follow me and I'll show you.

SAMANTHA
I'm not going anywhere. Rob's hurt
and needs our help.

TALL MAN
Oh, you patched things up did you?

SAMANTHA
Huh?

TALL MAN
It's a major complaint, seeing
things that aren't really there.

She turns and sees the tree, but the van and Rob are gone.

SAMANTHA
But he was right there.

TALL MAN
Like I said.

The tall man turns, walks toward the hedge. He turns back.

TALL MAN (CONT'D)
Coming?

They look at each other then agree to follow. He leads them through an opening in the hedge toward the Camp Nahgano road.

OTHER SIDE OF HEDGE

It's unbelievable. Everything is pristine with manicured hedges and lawns. The once faded welcome signs and giant arrows are being freshly painted by Native American CHILDREN.

Further up, Native American WOMEN and young GIRLS work the gardens and the older BOYS and MEN brush resin onto the logs of the lodge. Nobody speaks as they move in robotic fashion.

The tall man continues on, everyone follows taking it all in.

TOM
Wish I had my camera.

TALL MAN
No need for that. We're almost to
one thousand.

KEVIN
One thousand what?

Sam catches up to the Tall Man.

TALL MAN
(toward Samantha)
Oh, and you were a bonus.

SAMANTHA
What's that supposed to mean?

The tall man ignores her and continues walking.

SAMANTHA (CONT'D)
So, what is this place?

TALL MAN
Questions, questions. It's always who, what, where, why and when.

TOM
I think you forgot how?

TALL MAN
No. How, was up to you.

TOM
Huh?

SAMANTHA
So I'm dead?

No response. He continues leading them to the lodge entrance.

SAMANTHA (CONT'D)
Look, I saw my dead body. So, give it to me straight, is this Heaven?

He stops, LAUGHS hysterically.

TALL MAN
Heaven? Dear God, no!
(leaning in)
It's Camp Nahgano.

JULIE
What does that even mean?

TALL MAN
Nahgano. Nah Gonna know you're gonna die. Get it?

He breaks out in thunderous LAUGHTER.

JULIE
That's not what Kat said.

TALL MAN
Who's Kat? Me-ow (beat) oh, how rude of me. I almost forgot to introduce myself. I'm your host with the most. Teeth that is.

His wide mouth opens revealing hideously-jagged teeth. His lips continue to draw unnaturally back as more teeth push forward with tiny gears and blades that spin.

Everyone recoils backwards, shocked. He sucks his teeth back in, LAUGHING and glances at his fancy steam-punk watch.

TALL MAN (CONT'D)
(cheerful)
Oh, It's almost time. You're in for a real treat. Come, come.

They look at each other then reluctantly follow the tall man.

SAMANTHA
Time for what?

JULIE
Oh my God, did you see that?

TOM
And we're following him?

TALL MAN
Come, come. Everyone.

He stops, everyone stops. He points to a MAN who steadies himself up on the lodge roof, wraps a rope around his neck.

TOM
What's happening?

TALL MAN
Watch, this is the best part.

The tall man glances at his watch.

TALL MAN (CONT'D)
Three, two, one!

On (1), the man leaps off, SNAP of his neck. His lifeless body slams against the lodge, he dangles, dead.

TALL MAN (CONT'D)
Isn't it great. You all get to relive your death. Over and over and over. Bet you can't wait, hmm?

Off in the distance we hear someone screaming in pain, dying. A moment later, another one. The sounds are horrifying.

JULIE
I'm sorry, you're say'n I'm dead?

Chuck shows up with Halbert.

CHUCK
There you guys are. I've been looking all over. Oh, this is-

TALL MAN
Halbert! Get over here! You know the rules.

Halbert sheepishly joins the tall man. Chuck gives the tall man a once over.

TALL MAN (CONT'D)
Hello Chuck.

Chuck takes a step backwards.

TALL MAN (CONT'D)
The first to go, last to show. I'm wondering Chuck, do you like ants?

CHUCK
Is that a sick joke?

The tall man clasps his hands together, LAUGHING.

TALL MAN
Smashing!

INT. CAVE

Kat stands before the flickering flames, she waves the sage stick back and forth. The feather to her forehead. The dancing images and the drum beat continues.

KAT
Omis Ochee Hasse Taske.

The flames erupt with colors of green, blue and red. The fire intensifies. A distant RUMBLING is heard.

The Great Chief's image materializes in the fire once more.

GREAT CHIEF
Katrina, it is time to offer your blood and the fang, for this is our last chance.

She walks over to the stone wall, moves in close where two wolf fang indents are side-by-side in the stone. She looks back at the Great Chief in the flames.

KAT
Please, let my friends survive.

She removes the glowing wolf fang necklace, carefully snaps it into one of the two openings. SNAP! The fang glows GOLD.

EXT. CAMP NAHGANO - THE OTHER SIDE - AT THE SAME TIME

The ground begins to vibrate and rumble. The lodge sways. The emotionless people stop working.

The tall man instantly doubles over from a pain in his gut.

TALL MAN
Ooouugghh. Ooouugghh.

Still holding his gut, he looks around to everyone.

TALL MAN (CONT'D)
Get back to work!

He moves his hand away from his gut to reveal a black tar substance oozing out from inside him. He conceals it.

Samantha leans into Julie.

SAMANTHA
Something's wrong.

JULIE
This whole place is wrong.

TALL MAN
Back to work! We celebrate soon!

Everyone resumes working. He turns back toward the group.

TALL MAN (CONT'D)
You all come with me.

JULIE
We don't wanna go with you.

SAMANTHA
Yeah, we just wanna go home.

The tall man's face contorts into a hideous toothy fright.

TALL MAN
You are home.

He grabs Julie's arm, drags her toward the lodge.

TALL MAN (CONT'D)
I want you to have front row seats.

She kicks and drags her feet.

JULIE
I don't wanna front row seat.

Sam and Kevin rush to her aid when the tall man doubles over in pain releasing Julie. She stumbles to her friends, crying. They move further away from the doubled-over sick tall man.

INT. CAVE

Kat kneels before the fire as holograms of past leaders dance through the flames to the beat of the drums. With a small knife in hand, she slices her palm and drips blood into the fire. POOF! The flames become brilliant gold.

A Native American CHANT begins low but becomes louder, reverberating the walls. Dust and rocks crumble inside the cave. Kat raises her arms high. The violent shaking intensifies.

GREAT CHIEF
An okla, ulga!

KAT
An okla, ulga!

The words echo throughout the cave, over and over, louder and louder. The drums and chanting continue. The sound deafening. Kat covers her ears with her hands. Wolfdog runs out.

The wolf fang in the stone wall becomes brilliant gold. Instantly veins of light shoot up through the rocks and ceiling.

EXT. CAMP NAHGANO - AERIAL - NIGHT

An AERIAL view of the entire property as the ground and trees violently SHAKE.

The golden beam of light shoots upward from the ground just as the blue light beam from the glowing fang in Kevin's pocket shoots upward and they collide. CRASH!

As they collide a brilliant GREEN bolt of lightning smashes downward. Mushrooming and expanding like ripples in water. Starting at the lodge and moving outward like a synchronized circle of destruction. The CHANTING and DRUMS louder, faster.

Plumes of debris and dead ants geyser upward from every anthill on the property as if a mass cleansing is taking place. The lodge crumbles and groans.

EXT. CAMP NAHGANO ROAD - TREE - SAME

Rob, now propped up against a nearby tree has tied a cloth around his leg to stop bleeding. The ground SHAKES. He grabs onto the tree. EXPLOSIONS of ants and debris begin landing around him. Shielding himself, he hangs onto the tree.

INT. LODGE - SECOND FLOOR - CONTROL ROOM - SAME

The control room begins to crumble. The ceiling caves in, the gears and instruments spark and smoke. The scoreboard drops and crashes to the ground, still showing the number 999.

EXT. CAMP NAHGANO - THE OTHER SIDE - DAY

With destruction all around, the lodge crashes down. Souls of the people float upward into smokey shapes of sacred animals before disappearing into the stars. The tall man melts down to the size of a bug. His voice becomes higher as he goes.

TALL MAN

What's happening? This wasn't supposed to happen. I was almost there. Stop! Halbert! Help me!

Instantly a big shoe smashes down on him. SQUISH! PULL BACK to see it was Halbert's foot and he's happy about it.

HALBERT

I've waited a long time for that.

Everyone LAUGHS.

Instantly, Halbert begins to sparkle as he transforms into particles of light, lifting him, slowly moving upward.

HALBERT (CONT'D)
(excited)
I'm going up! I'm going uh-

POOF! His large particle of light floats upward.

Sam, Kevin, Chuck, Tom and Julie watch as hundreds of similar particles of light float upward. Magical.

KEVIN
Guess this is it.

He reaches out. They all hold hands.

JULIE
Don't say it like that.

CHUCK
Well at least we're all going up.

TOM
Don't count your chickens.

CHUCK
What does that even mean?

SAMANTHA
Please! Guys!

A tear rolls down her cheek.

SAMANTHA (CONT'D)
I love you guys.

They all move in for a group hug.

INT. CAVE

Kat stands before the fire, dancing images and the glowing fang when suddenly the fire is sucked out and the images gone. The drums, stop. It's quiet. The fang's light goes dim.

KAT
Chief? Chief are you there?

GREAT CHIEF (V.O.)
(echoing)
As promised, Princess Katrina.

KAT
Princess?

The fang's light intensifies a moment, catching the smokey image of the Great-Wolf rising from the pit. It shape-shifts into a HANDSOME MAN. He smiles, holds out his hand to her.

HANDSOME MAN
Daughter.

She reaches out, touches fingertips with him. Green sparks. He continues rising upward, smiling, proud.

KAT
Wait! Don't go!

He disappears into the ceiling of the cave. The fang's light goes dim once more. The cave now dark.

KAT (CONT'D)
What about my friends?

She snatches up the wolf fang necklace, puts it on just as wolfdog arrives and BARKS! He wants her to follow, she does.

EXT. CAMP NAHGANO ROAD - TREE - NIGHT

The shaking has stopped. Rob props himself up, painful. He reaches into his pocket and pulls from it his cellphone. Two percent battery left, no bars. He holds it up. No connection.

He drops his head, defeated.

EXT. CAMP NAHGANO - GATE ENTRANCE - NIGHT

Just inside the main road entrance where the strip of white powder crosses, lays a thick ribbon of dead ants. Then movement. A few ants emerge and escape the property through Chuck's boot-scuff in the white powder. They scurry away.

EXT. CAMP NAHGANO ROAD - TREE - SAME

Wolfdog leads Kat to the van and tree, passing mounds of dead ants. She rushes to Rob who is now slumped over.

KAT
Rob! Rob!

She feels for a pulse. He wakes up.

ROB
(disoriented)
Sam? Is that you?

KAT
Rob, it's me, Kat.

He focuses. He's weak.

ROB
Kat? You're alive!

He notices wolfdog.

ROB (CONT'D)
And you have a dog?

KAT
It's a long story but, where is everyone?

ROB
They're all dead.

KAT
NO!

She leaps up, rushes toward the van and sees Samantha on the ground. She kneels down, places two fingers on her neck, checks for a pulse. She instantly gets a vision. POW!

VISION

Just like someone's life flashing before their eyes, Kat sees the love and heroic actions her friends made trying to save one another, including their search for her. The vision ends on Samantha holding a positive pregnancy test strip.

Kat SNAPS BACK to reality, grabs and clutches the wolf fang around her neck. She quickly turns toward Rob, hopeful.

EXT. CAMP NAHGANO - GATE ENTRANCE - A SHORT TIME LATER

As if by magic, the van materializes on the road just outside the entrance to Camp Nahgano completely unscathed. POOF!

INT. VAN - DAWN

Everyone appears disoriented as they are now back in the van. Rob, shocked he's behind the wheel and not injured, looks over, sees Samantha and everyone in back. He slowly reaches over, pokes Sam's arm to see if she's real.

SAMANTHA
Ouch!

ROB
You *are* real. I think.

SAMANTHA
Of course I'm real. Right?

The van door slides open revealing Kat who stands just outside. Next to her, NATHAN 30s, the handsome Native American backpacker and his wolfdog, Tala.

ROB
I must be dreaming or dead.

KAT
You're neither.

Rob gives her a curious look.

KAT (CONT'D)
(toward Rob)
Think of it as a gift of gratitude from the Great Chief. Oh, this is Nathan Clearwater and you've already met Tala.

CHUCK
Great Chief? What's happening?

SAMANTHA
Oh I get it. We're all still dead like in that show, Lost.
(toward Rob)
But then you'd be dead.

TOM
Jesus Christ, that ending sucked.

CHUCK
The worst.

KAT
I can assure you, you're all very much alive.

TOM
Then why do I remember shit like me dying.

SAMANTHA
Yeah, and me - I saw my dead body.

JULIE
Did we die or not? And how the fuck are we back in the van?

KAT
Okay, yes, everyone died...

A collective GASP.

KAT (CONT'D)
...Except for me and Rob and Tala.

He looks at Sam, sad. Kat moves in closer to the open door.

KAT (CONT'D)
Okay, the abbreviated version. Nathan and I are the last of our people. We were summoned here to stop an evil entity but Nathan got killed before he could help. Then we show up. I fall into a cave, meet the Great Chief and with my blood and the ancient great spirits we were able to stop evil, free our people and as my reward you were all brought back to life. Oh and I think my dad's a mythical wolf and I'm a princess.

Everyone's dumbfounded.

TOM
Are you fucking kidding me?

JULIE
Strangely enough, I believe her.

CHUCK
Now who's been smoking?

KAT
It's the truth.

ROB
If I hadn't seen what I saw, I wouldn't believe it either but I do. Thank you, whatever you did.

Kat smiles, happy.

KEVIN
You know it's weird, I suddenly don't feel so afraid of ghosts.

TOM
Because you are one.

Kevin GASPS, looks for anything to see his reflection.

KEVIN
I am not. Am I??

Julie produces a small mirror, hands to Kevin.

JULIE
You're not a ghost.

ROB
(toward Nathan)
You look so familiar.

KEVIN
Oh my God, the dude from the tent.

NATHAN
I'm afraid so. Luckily, I was saved
by this beautiful goddess.

KEVIN
Wait a minute.

Kevin digs into his pocket, retrieves the fang necklace.

KEVIN (CONT'D)
I believe this belongs to you.

He hands it over to Nathan who becomes instantly excited.

NATHAN
Thank you. Thank you so much.

He quickly fastens it around his neck.

SAMANTHA
(toward Kat)
I can see why you saved him.

Kat blushes, then pulls Tom's camera from behind her back.

KAT
I know how much this meant to you.

TOM
(gasps)
My Sony H.X.R one hundred!

He grabs it, kisses it.

TOM (CONT'D)
Oh my God, we *are* alive!

Everyone LAUGHS. He turns toward Samantha.

TOM (CONT'D)
So, we still hooking up later?

SAMANTHA
Not a chance.

He SHRUGS then goes back to loving his camera.

CHUCK
Get a room.

They all LAUGH.

EXT. VAN - DAWN

Kat steps back from the open van door.

KAT
So with that, I want you to start
that engine Rob and get going.

JULIE
You're not coming?

KAT
Nah. This is where I belong.

SAMANTHA
Are you sure?

ROB
There's plenty of room in the van.

KAT
Thanks, but I'm staying.

Nathan puts his arm around Kat.

NATHAN
Now that the grounds are cleansed
we can rebuild. Start a family.

Kat smiles as she leans into the van door.

KAT
So don't be strangers.

Tom clutches his camera, securely.

TOM
Thank you for this, but no offense
I'm not coming back.

CHUCK
Yeah, me neither.

JULIE
I second that or, is it third?

Rob starts the engine. Kat slides the door shut and blows them a kiss.

EXT. CAMP NAHGANO - GATE ENTRANCE - SAME

The van pulls away down the road. Arms are waving out the windows as a collective "THANK YOU" is HEARD.

Kat, Nathan and Tala watch them go.

INT. VAN - FRONT SEATS

Rob drives the bumpy road heading away from Camp Nahgano.

ROB
This was a miracle. You guys know that, right?

BACK OF VAN

KEVIN
Easy for you to say, you didn't get your face bashed in.

JULIE
Yeah it sucks we remember.

CHUCK
I suppose we didn't get any of it on camera.

TOM
Don't look at me, I stopped filming the second I got ripped to shreds by bad wallpaper!

Tom snatches up his camera.

TOM (CONT'D)
Wait a minute.

He clicks it on.

TOM (CONT'D)
Let's see if I can show you guys what happened. There was a mirror across from me and I was filming..

Tom checks his camera feed.

EXT. VAN - SAME

As the van continues down the dirt-pavement road we hear-

JULIE (V.O.)
Ewe. Watch you die? That's gross.

CHUCK (V.O.)
Not as gross as being eaten alive by billions of fucking ants.

JULIE (V.O.)
Excuse me. I not only got eaten but I drowned in the river.

KEVIN (V.O.)
Um actually, you bled to death.

JULIE (V.O.)
Whatever.

INT. VAN - SAME

Julie opens her laptop.

JULIE
Yay! We have internet!

Everyone grabs their cellphones, checking.

TOM
(into his camera)
Holy shit. This is insane.

We HEAR ripping and screaming as Tom gets ripped apart.

SAMANTHA
Please turn that off.

ROB
Good to see we're back to normal.

TOM
Yo Chuck, check your recorder, we can use that shit. Can you imagine what our ratings will do?

JULIE
You guys didn't get me, did you?

KEVIN
I wish.

Julie slugs Kevin's arm.

Chuck rewinds his recorder, plays. Instantly, we HEAR the horrible sounds of him screaming while being eaten.

CHUCK
Nope. Nope. Not gonna hear this.

He stops the recording.

TOM
What are you doing? You always say you want the best sound effects and I'm telling you, that's the best creepy sound effect I've ever heard! Maybe not as good as mine...

KEVIN
Yeah dude, this shit's dope.

ROB (O.S.)
I have to agree.

JULIE
Actually, it's brilliant.

Julie turns her laptop toward everyone.

JULIE (CONT'D)
Look. We're already trending from the last episode. This one's gonna blow us up.

FRONT SEATS

Rob navigates the rough road, looks over toward Sam.

ROB
This is an interesting turn of events (beat) So what was it like?

SAMANTHA
Being dead? I could see you. Over by the van. And I could hear you.

ROB
No way, that's impossible.

SAMANTHA
You had a rod in your leg. You pulled it out and crawled over to-

ROB
Whoa, you did see me. And heard me?

SAMANTHA
Every single word.

ROB
Well then you know.

She places her hand on her belly, pats it, smiles.

SAMANTHA
It's okay, we can make it work.

Rob's eyes go WIDE, surprised.

EXT. CAMP NAHGANO - GATE ENTRANCE

A cloud of dust is all that remains as the van disappears down the road. Kat and Nathan turn back toward the property, she takes his hand. They look out over the land, hopeful.

CLOSE on Kat's eyes as they momentarily glow a greenish sparkle. She looks at the camera, SMILES.

CUT TO BLACK.

ROLL SOME CREDITS THEN-

FADE IN:

EXT. TEHACHAPI MOUNTAIN ROAD - DAY

The day seems brighter. As if a heavy burden has been lifted. An EAGLE soars past in the clear blue cloudless sky. An SUV towing a small fishing boat, makes its way up the road.

INT. SUV

STEVE and HELEN both 60s enjoy light conversation when a deer darts in front of them. Before Steve can react, they hit the deer, it falls injured off to the side.

The SUV jack-knives sending the boat careening over the edge. The SUV ROLLS several times before coming to rest on its roof. Helen and Steve dangle unconscious held by their seatbelts. Dust and broken glass settle around them.

She opens her eyes. Disoriented. She looks over to see Steve.

EXT. TEHACHAPI MOUNTAIN ROAD - AT THE SAME TIME

The injured deer attempts to move but before it can, it's quickly overtaken by the escaped flesh-eating ants. Within seconds the deer carcass is stripped clean.

INT. OVERTURNED SUV

Helen's eyes widen in horror as she watches this. She struggles with her seatbelt. Her freshly cut arm begins bleeding. Steve, still knocked out, dangles.

SLOW as a drip of blood from her arm falls and hits the pavement. As soon as it HITS, the ants notice.

FADE TO BLACK.

A DISEMBODIED SCREAM.

FADE OUT.

www.ingramcontent.com/pod-product-compliance
Lightning Source LLC
LaVergne TN
LVHW050320160826
845677LV00014B/3495

9798834994749